A
Third Class
Murder

By Hugh Morrison

D1390498

MONTPELIER PUBLISHING
2021

Published in Great Britain by Montpelier Publishing

ISBN: 9798588023917

A
Third Class
Murder

Chapter One

The Reverend Lucian Shaw, Vicar of All Saints' church, Lower Addenham, was having one of those rare moments when all felt right with the world.

It was a beautiful bright morning in early spring, and the sun streamed through the large windows of the dining room; the vicarage, although small and somewhat shabby, was a well-proportioned house which looked its best in sunlight; so much brighter and calming than some clerical houses he had known, steeped in Victorian Gothic gloom. A cheerful little fire burned in the small grate, and his wife Marion seemed in good spirits too.

'Will that be all, ma'am?' said the maid, as she set the breakfast things on the table in front of the vicar, a tall, slim man in fit middle age with a fine head of greying hair.

'Yes thank you, Hettie,' said Mrs Shaw with a smile, and Hettie bobbed quickly then disappeared into the kitchen.

Another thing to be thankful for, thought Shaw, as he accepted a cup of tea poured by his wife. Servants were so hard to come by these days and not only was Hettie efficient, she was polite as well.

His sermon for Easter Sunday was coming along well, and would be finished today; a pleasant trip to the nearby town of Great Netley to see the Rector there about the forthcoming Whitsun parade was also on the agenda for the day. His new curate, Laithwaite, just down from Cambridge, was, like Hettie, also proving to be refreshingly capable in his role.

As he spread some marmalade on a slice of toast, the brief moment of almost absolute contentment was broken by his wife.

'I see the Cokeleys have been arguing again'.

Shaw gave a brief sigh and a text sprang into his mind. Proverbs 18. 'Pride goeth before destruction, and a haughty spirit before a fall'. Well, he thought, he hadn't exactly been haughty this morning, but perhaps a little too self-satisfied.

He turned to his wife and smiled. 'Private domestic matters ought to be no concern of ours, my dear.'

'I know, Lucian,' said Mrs Shaw awkwardly. 'You know I'm not one to gossip, but...'

'...that "but", Marion, is generally the preamble of someone who *is* one to gossip.'

'I'm concerned, that's all. The air's so still this morning you could hear them all over the high street. I couldn't help noticing it when I took Fraser out for his walk.'

At the sound of his name and perhaps the word 'walk', the little white West Highland Terrier stood up from below the table and looked up at his mistress with bright eyes, wagging his tail. Mrs Shaw patted his head.

'What was it this time?' asked Shaw, not really wanting to know, but recognising his wife generally had his parishioners' best interests at heart.

'Money again,' replied Mrs Shaw. 'I could hear them talking quite loudly from the window above their shop and at one point they were almost shouting'.

Shaw smiled. 'I trust you were not eavesdropping?'

'Of course not,' said Mrs Shaw. 'I merely stopped to look at a few things in their shop window. They always have such lovely displays.'

Charles Cokeley and his wife ran a small antiques shop in the village; not a mere second-hand shop of the type found in many towns around East Anglia, but a well-kept place with some genuinely beautiful pieces on display.

The Cokeleys, as far as Shaw knew, were a respectable middle-aged couple in the village, and generally appeared friendly to one another when attending church or other functions. Neither had come to him with any problems, but his pastoral sixth-sense told him all was not well in their domestic life. This was now the second argument that had been overheard by his wife.

'Mrs Cokeley was saying something about it being high time they sold up and left the village,' continued Mrs Shaw.

'But he, I mean, Mr Cokeley, was not having any of it and was downright rude to her. He called her an awful name, which I shan't repeat, and said he wasn't moving and that was that. Ought we to say something, Lucian? I passed by one of the ladies from the Women's Institute and I'm certain she heard it as well, and there were two of the choirboys on their way to school sniggering as they passed.'

Shaw sighed. Perhaps because of his own happy domestic situation, he was reluctant to face the fact that many, if not even most, marriages had their rocky patches.

After a moment's pause, Shaw replied decisively. 'No, my dear. It is neither my place nor yours to interfere, unless and until one of them comes to me for guidance. For now, suffice it to remember them in your prayers.'

Mrs Shaw smiled gently at her husband. It was silly of her, she thought, to think he would wish to be troubled by village gossip. 'I will stop by the shop,' she said, 'and deliver the parish magazine. They do have some really lovely things in there.'

While the Shaws were taking their breakfast, a less harmonious domestic scene was taking place a short distance away, as a heavy-set, ruddy man, still in shirt-sleeves, stood talking to his over-dressed wife in the small parlour above their antiques shop on the high street.

'I still don't see why you can't accept the estate agents' offer. This place has been losing money for years and it's about time we sold up and tried somewhere new.'

This was said by Freda Cokeley, a woman who had been attractive in her youth but who was now showing the signs of middle-aged spread and white roots beneath her gaudy blonde hair.

Her husband, Charles Cokeley, glared at her. 'Perhaps if you got up off that sofa and helped me in the shop we'd have a bit more money,' he growled. 'We wouldn't have to pay Miss Ellis to help out, for a start.'

'I don't see why you need her anyway,' said his wife. 'It's not as if we're inundated with customers.'

'I've told you, I have to go on buying trips, don't I? And if you won't run the place while I'm gone, then someone has to.'

'Buying trips!' snorted Mrs Cokeley. 'Drinking trips, more like.'

Cokeley bridled. 'It's none of your damned business what they are.'

Mrs Cokeley stepped in front of her husband and glared at him. 'Close that window you great oaf, people will hear you all the way down the street!'

Cokeley turned swiftly despite his bulk, and slammed down the sash window which bounced in its frame with the impact.

'There,' he said, impatiently. 'Happy now?'

'Yes. If you must call me all the names under the sun then kindly don't do it when the vicar's wife is walking past along with half the village.'

'Damn the vicar's wife,' said Cokeley calmly, 'and damn you.'

'Well I like that,' said Mrs Cokeley, with a sharp intake of breath. 'And you reading the lesson and taking the plate round that church of a Sunday. Call me what you will but at least I'm not a hypocrite'.

'And what's that supposed to mean?' countered Cokeley, buttoning his waistcoat and checking his reflection in the glass above the chimney-piece. He smoothed a strand of hair across his balding pate until he was satisfied it was in the correct place.

'You know very well what I mean. Have a look at that board with the ten commandments on it next time you're in church and remind yourself of that one about adultery.'

'Don't be ridiculous. I'm a respectable married man.'

'Married you may be, my love, but there's nothing respectable about you.'

'Meaning?'

'Meaning I've seen the way you look at that Miss Ellis. Ever since she's been helping in the shop you've been gazing at her like a love-sick puppy. I dare say you'll be inviting her on one of your "buying trips" soon, if you haven't already.'

Cokeley snorted a laugh as he put on his jacket and walked to the stairs; it was almost time to open the shop.

'Her? You're imagining things. She's as plain as a brown

envelope, and about as flat, too.'

'Disgusting!' retorted Mrs Cokeley as she picked up the *Radio Times*, and prepared herself for a busy day on the sofa with the wireless and a box of Rowntree's chocolates for company. Her husband stomped down the stairs into the shop below. He had a few things to do before Miss Ellis arrived.

Sybil Ellis, 29, plain and drifting towards becoming an old maid, finished her frugal breakfast and began clearing away the plates. Her mother, grey-haired and crippled with arthritis, struggled to get up from the table.

'You stay there, mother. I don't want you having another fall.'

'Alright, I'll stay put,' said Mrs Ellis petulantly. 'I wouldn't want to be any bother. I just thought I'd do the dishes as you've got to go to work.'

'It's alright, mother. Leave them. I'll do them when I get back. Just don't go doing anything that means we have to get the doctor out again, as there's nothing to pay him with'.

'Money!' snorted Mrs Ellis. 'Root of all evil, that is. Common even to talk about it, if you ask me.'

Miss Ellis sighed as she looked around the back kitchen of the small gimcracked house; the flat outhouse roof had been leaking again, and she knew the landlord wouldn't do anything about that as they were behind with the rent.

Money had been tight since her father had died, his small retirement nest egg exhausted by doctors' bills and then the costs of the 'big send-off' her mother insisted had to be organised. Any attempts at economy were considered 'common' by Mrs Ellis, and she had no idea of the perilous situation the family was in.

A pauper's funeral had been her father's lifelong fear, thought Miss Ellis; never mind the fact she'd ended up little better than a pauper herself, having had no time for courting either, while attending to her father in his last illness.

Her brother Jack pushed back his chair and lit a Gold Flake cigarette, exhaling a long stream of smoke with a satisfied sigh. He never let much bother him and seemed to drift from job to job; at present he had a somewhat precarious place on the railways, but Miss Ellis did not expect him to keep it long.

'You'll remember to give me housekeeping this week, won't you, Jack?' said Miss Ellis as she picked up her hat and gloves. 'Don't go spending it all on beer and the pictures again.'

'Don't nag, sis!' said Ellis cheerily. 'You'll get every brass farthing, to keep us in the style to which we're accustomed. Beats me why you need my cash anyway, what with that job you've got in King Tut's Palace.'

'King Tut's Palace' was Ellis' nickname for Cokeley's antique shop.

'Urgh' shuddered Miss Ellis. 'That place. Gives me the creeps and so does he. Soon as I can get something better, I will. When this awful slump's over I might be able to find something better. Or some one.'

Mrs Ellis took note of this. 'You could do worse than that employer of yours,' she said. 'That Mr Cokeley. He must be worth a pretty penny.'

'He's married, mother,' said Miss Ellis.

Mrs Ellis, who although unable to get out much nonetheless retained a keen interest in local gossip, gave a toothless smile. 'I know he's married, but not for much longer, from what I've heard. Fight like cat and dog, those two do. Something will happen before long, mark my words. Then's your chance.'

'Oh yes, something such as what?' asked Miss Ellis.

'Such as a...'

Here Mrs Ellis paused, not wanting to utter out loud the shocking word. She decided to spell it out euphemistically instead.

'Such as a D. O. R. V. I. C. E.'

Ellis laughed. 'A door vice, mother? What's one of those then?'

'Quiet,' barked Mrs Ellis. 'You know what I'm talking about.'

Miss Ellis shuddered. 'Even if he was divorced I wouldn't want him. He's an old goat and a brute and his wife's not much better.'

Mrs Ellis cackled. 'Maybe he's not such a good bet, then. His wife might do away with him before he gets a chance to leave her.'

'That's not funny, mother', said Miss Ellis, 'And I've got to go to work now.' She stepped into the narrow, gloomy vestibule and adjusted her hat in the hall-stand mirror.

Ellis stood beside her and put his cap on; with his slight build and delicate features, there was little difference between the faces of the two siblings in the sepulchral light of the corridor.

Lowering her voice so that her mother could not hear from the parlour, Miss Ellis turned to her brother. 'All set?'

He opened the front door and nodded decisively. 'All set, sis. Let's go.'

The Reverend Shaw strolled along the high street, dawdling a while; Laithwaite was reading Morning Prayer at the church today so he had some free time before he was due to visit the Rector at Great Netley.

Perhaps, he thought, after hearing his wife's concerns about the Cokeleys, a visit to their shop might be a harmless first step. A 'recce', they had called it in the war; a spying out of the land before engaging. He really did not wish to interfere in his parishioners' private lives, but at the same time, felt a strong sense of duty toward them; if he provided a presence to those in need, they could ask for counsel if they wished it; if they did not, he had at least been there for them. Besides, his wife's birthday was not far off, and it would do no harm to browse for a small gift.

Shaw approached the old shop, with its bottle-glass bow-fronted window and overhanging upper storey. The sash window which had been the oracle of gossip was now firmly closed.

Seeing nothing of interest in the window, he entered the shop, inhaling the smell of ancient wood and wax polish. No bell rang, nor did there appear to be anybody at the counter.

He looked around at the bewildering display of objects, all with their little price tags, covering almost every inch of the shop. He wondered how on earth anyone could keep track of them all. He noticed some Victorian watercolours of Norfolk hanging on the wall of an alcove in a far corner, and remembering that Mrs Shaw had a particular love of that neighbouring county, he walked over to view them more closely.

Just then, the door opened, and Shaw noticed Albert Goggins limping into shop, pausing for a moment to catch his breath. Shaw recognised him as an occasional attender at the church, who organised the annual Armistice Day service.

'Shop!' called Goggins impatiently, while he twirled his white moustaches; a former warrant officer in the army, he was not one to mince his words when requesting something.

Shaw had been about to greet him, but something in the man's tone made him keep his place in the gloom of the alcove.

Stepping forward to the counter, he rapped his stick on the polished surface and called out again. 'Anyone there?'

Cokeley appeared from the small back room, looking as if he had been exerting himself in some way. His professional shopman's smile faded slightly as he realised who it was who had called.

'Oh, it's you, Mr Goggins. Good morning to you.'

Goggins nodded curtly. 'Morning. Well?'

Cokeley smiled. 'Very well, thank you. And you?'

'Don't play silly beggars, Cokeley. I mean well what about it?'

'What about what?'

'You know what. The offer. Any thoughts?'

Cokeley's expression returned to that of feigned professional courtesy. 'Ah, of course. You mean the items you brought in for valuation. I've had a chance to look them over but the offer still stands, same as when I told you when you brought them in.'

Just then a slightly built, plain young woman in horn-rimmed spectacles and a shapeless tweed suit walked into the shop. Shaw recognised her as Cokeley's shop assistant.

'Good morning Mr Cokeley,' she said in an expressionless voice.

'Oh good morning, Miss Ellis,' said Cokeley. 'You're just

in time to return some goods to this gentleman. Fetch that cardboard box from the back room please, the one by the desk'.

A moment later Miss Ellis placed the box on the counter, with a metallic clink. She stood beside Cokeley impassively as he began listlessly fingering through the contents.

'Things like this don't fetch much these days,' said the dealer.

'Every blasted junk shop owner since Adam has said that, I'll wager,' said Goggins irritably.

'They may well have done, Mr Goggins,' said Cokeley, 'but since I sell antiques this is not a junk shop.'

'You buy junk and sell antiques, is what you mean', snorted Goggins. 'So you're not budging on the price then?'

'No,' said Cokeley decisively. 'Ten shillings is a fair price for nick-nacks like this'.

'Nick-nacks!' exploded Goggins. 'That's military history!' He started taking items out of the box and slamming them on the counter, unwrapping them from their protective layers of newspaper. 'That's my father's medals from Balaclava. And that's a German bayonet that my lads had engraved for me in the South African war. And that's a letter my grandfather got from Wellington after Waterloo. And those are my medals – *my* blasted medals – and you know that lot's worth more than ten shillings.'

Shaw, observing all this, realised he was in an awkward situation; unable to leave without attracting attention, he was now guilty of eavesdropping. He held his place in the corner, hoping for an opportunity to leave without being noticed.

'Military memorabilia really isn't worth much these

days,' said Cokeley, airily. 'People have had enough of war since the last lot. Ten shillings, cash. Take it or leave it.'

'Then I'll damned well leave it!' exclaimed Goggins. 'Pardon me, miss,' he added, with a nod to Miss Ellis.

A woman, who Shaw recognised out of the corner of his eye as Mrs Cokeley, entered from the back parlour.

'What's all this noise?' she said. 'I can barely hear the wireless upstairs'.

'Nothing my dear,' said Cokeley. 'Mr Goggins was just leaving. Be so kind as to help Miss Ellis pack these things away, would you?'

'Anyone would think I'm the hired help,' said Mrs Cokeley. 'Well, since I'm here I suppose so.'

Miss Ellis and Mrs Cokeley were absorbed in wrapping the items in newspaper and returning them to the box, watched over by Goggins, while Cokeley stood with his back to the shop, pretending to be interested in a minor adjustment to a cuckoo clock on the wall.

Shaw spotted his chance to escape and backed deftly to the door. Miss Ellis gave the box to Goggins, who struggled slightly to balance it in front of him. He turned and saw Shaw framed in the doorway.

'Morning vicar,' said Goggins. 'Didn't hear you come in. You're just the man I need to see.'

'Good morning, Mr Goggins,' said Shaw. 'And what did you wish to see me about?'

'When's the next sale of works?'

'Sale of works?'

'Yes, you know,' said Goggins, in a voice tinged with sarcasm. 'The next church jumble sale.'

'In about a month's time, I believe,' said Shaw, unclear as to why he was being asked.

'Good,' said Goggins. 'Then you can have this lot.' He nodded towards the box in his arms. 'This old swindler

Cokeley here says they aren't worth more than ten shillings. Well if that's all they're worth, then I reckon you might as well have them to raise money for the roof fund. They might even fetch more, if anyone with a bit of Christian charity is left in this village.'

Before Shaw could answer, he had the box thrust firmly into his arms by Goggins, who then pulled open the door violently.

Turning to face Cokeley behind the counter, he added loudly 'and that box is not the only thing in this place that I'd like rid of!'

Turning back to Shaw, he nodded and said 'good day to you, vicar', then stomped out of the shop.

Frank Symes, property developer and estate agent, lit his first cigarette of the day and leaned back in his modernist office chair, smoothing his brilliantined hair and running a finger along the pencil moustache on his rather ratty face.

His partner Joe Davis, a short, round-faced man who handled the sales side of things, was at his desk on the opposite side of the office, engrossed in a telephone call. Their secretary, Ruth Frobisher, sat with a bored expression at the reception desk, idly filing her nails and pausing occasionally to stare out of the window.

The office, at the bottom end of Lower Addenham's high street, was little more than a shed on the edge of a field. Next to it, facing the road, was a large sign depicting a pastoral scene of a smiling family emerging from a Morris saloon car into the driveway of a mock-tudor semi-detached house with an immaculately kept garden.

Above it were painted the words, in a typeface more suited to a cinema foyer than a rustic village: *Live the Country Life in New Addenham for just £50 down.*

This billboard was reproduced in smaller size on the wall behind Symes' desk.

Other pictures on the walls showed the various types of houses that were to form part of the estate of New Addenham; there was the Tudorbethan, in detached or semi-detached; the Hathaway Bungalow with art-deco stained glass door, and, Symes' favourite, the Hollywood Mexican Moderne, with its gleaming white walls, green tiled roof and curved Crittal steel windows.

'Yes sir, that's right,' said Davis to a customer on the telephone. He continued his rapid sales patter. 'Fifty pounds down for the Hathaway or the Shakespeare bungalow, then a pound a week for ten years at five per cent, and the fresh country air is free of charge.'

Davis looked over at Symes and winked, making a thumbs-up sign. 'Yes sir, do call in, yes we look forward to seeing you. Good day to you, sir'.

Davis replaced the receiver in its cradle. 'That's another interested party, Symie my boy,' he said, clapping his hands together and rubbing them. 'Won't be long before we get our first sale, and once this lot's gone we'll be off and doing it somewhere else. Symes and Davis houses from here to London.'

'You can certainly talk the talk, Joe,' said Symes, turning a fountain pen over in his fingers, 'and I hate to keep a good man down, but you're forgetting one thing. We can't sell anything until old king Cokeley sells up.'

'I still don't understand what the problem is with him,' said Davis.

'Look, I'll explain it to you again,' replied Symes. He turned to Miss Frobisher, who was now primping her blonde hair while looking at herself in a small compact mirror. 'Ruth, sweetheart, get me the file on Cokeley, will you?'

Miss Frobisher looked up with a start. 'Cokeley? Is that the stout party that's been in here a few times?'

'That's the one,' said Davis. 'Runs the old junk shop up the road.'

'Oh, him,' said Miss Frobisher with a shudder. 'Undresses me with his eyes, does that one'.

Davis laughed. 'How does that work, then? I thought most men used their hands.'

Miss Frobisher scowled. 'Oh leave off Joe. I don't mind men looking at me, but only the ones *I* like'.

Symes sighed. 'Dear oh Lord. I know we pay you mainly to be a bit of window dressing but you can at least pick up a file and pass it over, can't you? There's a good girl.'

Miss Frobisher stood up, loudly extracted a file from the metal cabinet, and sauntered over to Symes' desk, where she slapped it down with such force that his empty teacup rattled in its saucer.

Symes raised his eyes heavenward and unfolded some plans from the file, as Davis came over to his desk.

'It's all to do with his property, see', said Symes, tracing his finger along the plans until he came to the outline of the shop. 'His old junk shop is right in the middle of where we need to build the access road to the estate. But he's refusing to sell.'

'I know all that,' said Davis, 'he keeps coming in here and agreeing then upping the price. But I still don't understand why we need to build the road exactly there. I'm a good salesman – my life, I could sell sand to the Arabs, not that I'm likely to meet any round here – but a town planner I am not.'

'If we knock down Cokeley's shop we can build a short

access road onto the estate,' replied Symes. 'That means it's only five minutes' walk from the station. We can't knock down any other properties because they're in a long line and we'd have to buy up the lot. Cokeley's is detached so it's the only one we need to get rid of'.

'It's only a row of old houses, not the blooming Maginot Line,' quipped Davis. 'Why can't we just build a road around them?'

'Because then you're extending the road nearly a mile from the station,' said Symes wearily. 'Not only do you have to pay for all that to be built, it adds to the journey time for commuters. Twenty minutes' walk to the station instead of five. That means they can't get to work in Norwich or even Ipswich in less than an hour because there's no direct trains from here.'

'Won't they all have motor cars?' asked Davis.

'Don't be daft,' said Symes. 'I know some of the houses have garages, but that's mostly for show. To make them feel like the they're the sort of people who can afford a motor car. But with the amount we're charging them they'll be lucky to have enough left over for a bicycle.'

Symes chuckled at his own joke and continued. 'No, they've got to be able to get to the station easily. So unless we build that road, the only buyers will be the local yokels and they haven't got two pennies to rub together.'

'Alright, I get it now,' said Davis, frowning. 'The old blighter's got us over a barrel, hasn't he?'

'He has indeed,' replied Symes. 'With all the money we've, or rather, *I've*, invested in this project, we've had it if we can't get our hands on that land.'

'Well I'm not giving up yet,' said Davis. 'If you think I'm going to go back to collecting rents in the Old Kent Road, you can think again. There's lots of people we owe money to and some have persuasive methods of getting it.'

An idea struck Symes. 'What day is it?'

'Wednesday, why?' said Davis.

'Didn't we try to get old Cokeley in here for a meeting last Wednesday and he wasn't having it, said something about always going in to Great Netley for lunch at the King's Head on a Wednesday?'

'Cor blimey, you want I should be his social secretary now?' replied Davis in an annoyed tone.

'No, he's right,' replied Miss Frobisher, not looking up from filing her nails. 'I remembering him saying it. Wednesday's half-day closing here, not that you two slave drivers take any notice of it'.

'Right then,' said Symes with an enthusiastic smile. 'Today's half-day closing for us as well. We go into Great Netley, go to the King's Head and see if we can't buy the old miser a few drinks and win him over.'

'Well…alright,' said Davis uncertainly.

'That's a date, then,' said Symes. 'But if that doesn't get him to sell up, we're going to have to think of something that will solve the problem of Mr Cokeley for good.'

Chapter Two

Shaw was in his study, seated at his battered roll-top desk. He was going over his notes for his lunch meeting with William Soames, Rector of Great Netley, concerning the joint Whitsun services and procession.

The custom of a large procession to celebrate Pentecost had been falling off in recent years, and so it had been decided to combine the work of the two parishes, holding a service in Great Netley and then processing to Lower Addenham for another service followed by a Sunday School tea for the children, who would undoubtedly be tired after the four-mile walk.

Shaw paused and looked out of the window of his small study at the daffodils on the neat front lawn of the vicarage. Beyond them on the lane he noticed a young man bicycling past; he tried to place him but could not, and reflected with a tinge of guilt that he always felt a little more comfortable with the administrative work of the parish than with attempting to remember the names and faces of his flock.

Events, meetings, services, these were predictable and satisfying, but people were sometimes...difficult, he concluded, and the scene he had witnessed at Cokeley's shop this morning only confirmed that. He glanced down at the cardboard box full of Goggins' war mementoes, making a mental note to ask their owner if he really had meant what he said about donating them. Unsure of their true value, he locked them in the battered Georgian cabinet by his desk, as a precaution against the highly unlikely event of the vicarage being robbed.

His thoughts were interrupted by a timid knock at the door. After Shaw had said 'come in', Hettie bobbed in the doorway .

'Please sir, there's a gentleman to see you.'

Shaw turned in his chair. 'Does this gentleman have a name, Hettie?'

Hettie blushed. 'Sorry sir. Yes sir, it's Mr Goggins'.

'Very good,' said Shaw. 'Send him in, please.'

Hettie bobbed and stepped aside into the little hallway. 'Send him in', thought Shaw, was a trifle pretentious an order for a house of these proportions, when the visitor could obviously hear what was going on, but he could never think of a better alternative.

Goggins stepped into the study and nodded at Shaw, who stood up to shake his hand.

'Morning again, vicar,' said Goggins. 'I'm sorry you had to witness that little scene in the shop earlier.'

Shaw waved his hand as if to dismiss the matter. 'Won't you sit down, Mr Goggins?'

'No thank you, I'll be brief. I meant what I said about those things.'

'Things, Mr Goggins?'

'Mementoes. Old war relics. Junk, as Cokeley would call it. I meant what I said. You can have them for the next jumble sale.'

'Ah yes,' said Shaw. 'I have just locked them away for safe keeping. Some fascinating things...a letter from the Duke of Wellington, no less.'

'That's right. Given to my grandfather. Got injured at Waterloo, right next to the Duke's entourage.'

'But Mr Goggins,' ruminated Shaw, 'these things may be valuable. Are you certain you want them sold for a few shillings at a church jumble sale?'

'I'm a man of my word, vicar, and I meant what I said in the shop, the church can have them. It might remind that fellow Cokeley about the camel and the eye of the needle.'

Shaw smiled at the reference to the biblical verse concerning avarice. He then decided to broach a difficult subject.

'Forgive me, Mr Goggins, I don't mean to pry, but may I ask why you were trying to sell the items?'

Goggins cleared his throat. 'I'd be lying if I told you I was just having a clear out, vicar. Fact is, things haven't been going so well lately, not since my wife died, and I could do with a bit of money coming in.'

'You're a saddler by trade, I believe?'

'Yes sir, that's right. Saddler and bridle maker. It's a dying trade, what with more motor cars on the roads every year, but I'm too old to learn another. Horses is my life, always has been.'

There was an awkward pause, broken by Shaw. 'Well, if I can be of assistance in any way…'

'I don't want charity,' said Goggins firmly. 'I just want a fair crack at the whip. That Cokeley, well, trying to sell me short on those mementoes, that was the last straw. He owns my cottage as well, see, and he was talking about turning me out because I couldn't pay the rent. I suppose I just snapped.'

Shaw took out his pipe and filled it slowly with his favourite Three Nuns tobacco, smiling as he remembered the lads in the trenches, back when he was a chaplain. 'There's the padre again enjoying himself with his three nuns,' they'd joke, but it was all good natured. The Western Front seemed a world away now from the petty problems of a small English village.

'I'll have a think,' said Shaw. 'There might be something we can find for you. The diocese has some cottages to rent over at Great Netley, I believe. I'll ask around.'

Goggins gave what passed for a smile. 'That's very kind of you, vicar.' He glanced at the long-case clock in the corner of the room. 'Oh that reminds me, I'd best be off. I'm due in Great Netley this afternoon, the dairy wants some new bridles. I'll need to get the next train, the 12.55.'

Shaw put his unlit pipe into his pocket. 'Good heavens, I'd clean forget that I'm due in Netley as well. I have a meeting with Mr Soames at half past one. Shall we walk to the station together?'

'It would be a pleasure, vicar,' said Goggins. 'Bridles for dairy horses,' he muttered, shaking his head. 'I used to make saddles for the Household Cavalry, and now I'm kitting out milkmen'.

Shaw smiled as he held open the door for Goggins to collect his hat from Hettie.

'Reg! Reg!' called Mrs West up the gloomy staircase to her son, who was sprawled out on his crumpled bed in the little back bedroom of the cramped terraced house in the cathedral city of Midchester, a few miles from Lower Addenham.

'What is it now, ma?' said the young man.

'Ain't you never getting out of that bed, boy?' continued his mother, yelling from the tiny hallway below. 'I wants to do out that room and you wants to go and get a job.'

'And you wants to put a bleeding sock in it and leave me be,' said West under his breath. 'Alright ma,' he yelled. 'Just give me five minutes.'

He got out of bed and pulled on his shabby trousers, shrugging the braces over his long woollen combinations, then buttoned up his shirt. He tied a scarf round his neck to hide his lack of a collar and tie, and put his ill-fitting suit jacket on. He decided not to bother shaving, and just combed his hair instead, looking at his reflection in the cracked piece of mirror on the wall above the narrow bedroom fireplace.

The mirror frame held a few yellowing pictures of film stars cut from newspapers. They had been there for at least five years, since before he'd been sent to prison. From what he'd seen since he'd got out, girls didn't look so much like that now, and the films themselves had changed beyond all recognition.

He'd heard inside from the newer lags about the 'talkies' but didn't believe it himself. How could people talk in a film? That was like expecting a gramophone record to start showing pictures as it spun round. The only sound he'd ever heard in a cinema was the same old four or five tunes banged out by the pianist at the local flea-pit.

So the first thing he'd done when he got out, before he'd even visited Maisie's, the little knocking-shop down by the slaughterhouse, was to treat himself to a visit to the big new picture palace in Midchester city centre.

Blow me, he thought, it was true about the talking pictures; beautiful girls with blonde hair talking on and on in exotic American accents, with jazz music playing, or posh English women who said things like 'terribly' and 'awfully' all the time. Not like the girls down at Maisie's, with their yokel voices. The best you got from them was 'How's you, my lover?' in a Suffolk drawl.

Thinking about it, that was what really decided it for him. No going straight for him. That was for losers. He decided that right there and then, as he nipped out of the picture house just in time to avoid having to stand for the national anthem.

No waiting in the queue at the labour exchange in the rain for him, with all those stupid sods too downtrodden to care any more. He was going back to his old life of crime, and that was going to be his ticket to the world of blonde girls who said 'terribly' and 'awfully' and 'frightfully'. He put his cap on and stomped down the stairs out into the street, slamming the door behind him.

Lower Addenham village station was one of those little backwaters of the London and North Eastern Railway that seemed to have changed little since it was built in the 1850s. It was the only stop on the branch line from Great Netley, just four miles long including a turning loop, a vanity project financed by the Earl of Addenham to enable weekend guests to visit more easily from London.

Traffic had always been light on the line and with advent of bicycles and then motor cars and buses, the number of passengers using the shuttle service each day had dwindled to single figures.

Shaw bought his ticket from the little window in the combined waiting room and ticket office, and walked through the overly ornate Victorian Gothic doors onto the platform; Goggins followed slowly. His usual limp, Shaw had noticed, had become more pronounced on the five minute walk to the station.

'Afternoon vicar, Mr Goggins,' said Ned Allen, the

station porter, touching his cap in a semi-salute in respect to the social status of the clergyman. 'You're a bit early gentlemen,' he added, checking the tickets of the two men, 'but we'll be off in just a few minutes.'

Shaw and Goggins sat down to wait on a bench, sandwiched between a row of milk crates and the station cat, asleep on one end of the seat.

Shaw took out his pipe and tamped down the tobacco with his thumb, applied a match to the bowl and sat back contendedly. Even if his country parson's stipend had stretched to running a motor car, he would not have been tempted to buy one; the train connected him with anywhere he wanted to go, and for local visits to parishioners, there was always his bicycle.

The little shuttle train was standing at the station's only platform, wisps of steam emerging from the underside of the little pannier-tank engine, as the driver and fireman tinkered about with oil cans and rags.

At one time the line had used a bigger engine, three coaches and a brake van, but passenger numbers were now so few that the service was reduced to a single coach, with four compartments, all third class, with a guard's section at the rear of the carriage.

The locals nicknamed it the 'toy train' which was of course incorrect, thought Shaw, as it was of the standard gauge, but he could see why they did so. From a distance the little engine and its one carriage, set against the vast East Anglian skies, looked more like the type of narrow gauge train one might see in the foothills of Wales.

The steam hissed and somebody cleared his throat. The guard stepped out of his small section at the rear of the train's only carriage, and began opening the compartment doors, calling out 'Great Netley service, all aboard please.'

Goggins stood up and Shaw noticed a twinge of pain in

his face for an instant. 'If it's all the same to you, vicar, I'll go in the non-smoking compartment. My lungs is playing up today.'

'My dear fellow,' said Shaw, apologetically, 'You should have mentioned it. Let me put this pipe out.'

'No, no, you keep it lit, vicar,' said Goggins. 'Never waste a smoke if you've got one – you'll remember that from the army, I expect. I'll be seeing you,' he added, as he stepped up awkwardly into one of the two compartments marked 'non-smoking' on the window. 'Give my regards to Reverend Soames.'

'I will do, Mr Goggins, and good day to you,' said Shaw as he opened the door to the smoking compartment. The sounds of escaping steam from the engine increased in volume as he sat back in the seat nearest the door. Although the compartment was designed to seat ten persons, five on either side between the two doors with their pull-down windows, he had it to himself, and so puffed away on his pipe with happy abandon.

Through the open window he heard rapid footsteps and the voices of two men, both speaking with London accents.

'Come on Joe, get a move on, the train's about to leave!' said one.

'Alright, alright,' replied the other, 'we wouldn't have had to rush if you'd get that company car I keep asking you to buy, Symie you old skinflint!'

Shaw heard a door slam and then muffled voices as the two men continued their good-natured argument.

He then observed a stout man move deftly across the platform towards the train, carrying an old brown Gladstone bag; he glimpsed the man's face and realised it was Cokeley. For the second time that day, Shaw drew back into the shadows to avoid recognition, then muttered a prayer of contrition. It seemed however that Cokeley had not recognised him, and he walked on to the door of the neighbouring compartment, nearest to the guard's section.

Shaw now heard the guard's voice. 'I've kept the compartment free for you, Mr Cokeley, as usual.'

Then Cokeley's voice: 'Thanks Bill. Here you are.' There was a sound of clinking coins.

'Thank you very much sir, and good day to you,' replied the guard.

Just then Shaw saw, briefly, a woman cross the platform. He had a glimpse of platinum blonde hair, dark glasses, a chiffon scarf and a figure of the type that men, even married clergyman, would definitely notice. An instant later and she was out of view, but he heard the guard admonishing her.

'I'm sorry miss, but this compartment's reserved.'

Then Shaw heard Cokeley reply in a somewhat oily tone. 'That's alright Bill, there's plenty of room. You step inside miss. Let me take your bag for you. That's right. Have a seat next to me by the window, why don't you?'

The door then slammed and Shaw could hear nothing more except the shrill of the guard's whistle and a responding blast of steam from the engine as it moved slowly out of the little station towards Great Netley.

Shaw sat back and puffed happily on his pipe, admiring the scenery along the line, particularly the trees with their stippling of green buds waiting to burst forth into leaves. This was his favourite time of year, he thought, as new life came forth in its annual miracle, anticipating the greatest miracle of all which would soon be celebrated at Easter.

The train picked up speed on a long straight stretch, the carriage beginning a rhythmic rattle which, on a longer journey, was likely to have lulled Shaw to sleep. This grew in volume until he noticed a strange sound – a cry, perhaps, from somewhere on the train. Dismissing it as some noise from the engine, his thoughts turned to the administrative challenges of the forthcoming Whitsun pageant.

The train began to slow down and, with much hissing of steam, eventually came to a standstill. Shaw looked up, thinking this somewhat unusual, but remembering that this was where the train joined the main London to Norwich line; an express would probably be passing and the small local train was obliged to stop at a signal. Just then, he heard the sound of a compartment door slamming and a crunch of gravel from a heavy impact. He then heard a voice from the rear of the train – presumably that of the guard – calling out.

'Hi, you, you can't do that! Get back inside!'

Shaw pulled down the window of the compartment door on his left, and looked out. He saw a figure in a dark suit and cloth cap, clutching what appeared to be a bag or bags, running first towards the engine and then left towards the signal on the side of the track. The figure then dropped one of the bags which rolled down into some undergrowth. He paused for an instant, half-turned around to look for the bag, but then carried on running and disappeared into the clump of bushes in front of the signal post.

Turning to look towards the rear of the train, Shaw saw the guard leaning out of the window of his section. He then heard a shout from the direction of the engine.

'Everything alright, Bill?'

'Just some darned fool jumping off the train,' replied the guard. 'Probably trying to dodge having his ticket checked at Netley.'

'I thought I saw someone jump out,' called the voice again from the direction of the engine, which Shaw assumed must be that of the driver. 'Some folk will do anything to save a few pence.'

Shaw heard a distant 'clunk' and looked up the line to his left to see the signal arm moving.

'That's us clear to go now Bill,' called the driver. 'We'd better get a move on or we'll miss the slot at Netley.'

'Carry on then,' yelled the guard.

The hissing of steam increased in volume again, and Shaw withdrew his head into the compartment, pulling up the window behind him.

A few minutes later the train pulled into the small market town of Great Netley. Shaw knocked out his pipe into the little ashtray by the door and took down his briefcase from the luggage rack. Stepping out onto the platform he nodded to Goggins who climbed out awkwardly from the train, holding tightly to the open door to support himself. The two London businessmen stepped out of their compartment. Shaw then noticed that not all the compartment doors had opened. Cokeley's was still closed.

The guard was walking the short length of the train, calling out 'Great Netley, all change, Great Netley, all change' in a booming voice. Shaw smiled as it seemed a little theatrical for a single carriage train on a branch line. Perhaps, he thought, the man had missed his calling as an actor. Shaw closed the door of his compartment behind him and felt in his pocket for his ticket in order to present it at the gate.

The guard glanced through the window of Cokeley's compartment and opened the door. 'Great Netley, all change! Come along now sir, wake up, wake up...Dear God!'

The guard half stepped, half fell backwards out of the compartment, knocking into Shaw as he passed.

'My dear fellow...' Shaw instinctively began to

apologise for being bumped into, in that peculiarly English way, when he looked through the open door into the compartment and saw Cokeley.

Shaw only needed one glance at the man, who lay slumped in his seat with the handle of a knife protruding from his chest, to know that he would not be waking up again until Judgement Day.

Chapter Three

The constable on point duty outside Great Netley station had acted quickly, instructing the station master to telephone for reinforcements and sealing off the platform, barring entry to the growing crowd of concerned onlookers and preventing anyone who had been on the train from leaving the station.

Within fifteen minutes of receiving the telephone call, Detective Inspector George Ludd from Midchester central police station arrived, the tyres of his Morris Six screeching slightly as his sergeant, James McPherson, braked heavily.

'Calm down, McPherson,' said Ludd, leaning over to switch off the car's electric bell. 'Sounds like there's been enough drama here for one day.'

'Sorry sir,' said the Scotsman breathlessly as the two men exited the car, 'but a murder! That's not something you get every day round these parts. I can't remember the last time we had one.'

'We don't know it's murder,' admonished Ludd. 'All we know is a man's been found dead.'

'Aye, but dead with a knife through the heart, the despatcher said.'

'Keep an open mind,' replied Ludd. 'First rule of detection. Things aren't always what they seem.'

Ludd and McPherson were met at the door of the station by the station master, a police constable and a third man with a black bag and a stethoscope around his neck.

Ludd nodded to the constable and introduced himself. 'Inspector Ludd, Midchester CID. You the one that called it in?'

The young officer saluted. 'Yes sir, glad you could get here so quick.'

'Got a name, lad?' replied Ludd.

'Yes sir. Jessop sir.'

'Right then Jessop. We'll take over from here. Go with the rest of this lot here.' He pointed to the dozen or so officers arriving in the station forecourt in two black vans. 'Seal all this area off. Don't let anyone in or out of the station.'

'You can't do that, I've got the London train coming through in a minute!' said a little man nearby.

'And who are you?' asked Ludd brusquely of the uniformed official.

'Albert Perkins, station master,' said the man, drawing himself up to his full height of five feet three inches. 'I can't close off the whole station as the London train's coming through in three minutes. That would be against regulations'.

'I think my regulations are bigger than your regulations, Mr Perkins,' said Ludd wearily.

'There's no need to close the whole station anyway,' said Perkins. 'The, er, the deceased party is on platform three, that's on its own down the end, nobody could have got on or off down there or we'd see 'em come through.'

'Alright then,' said Ludd, 'you can keep the rest of the place open but nobody comes in or out of platform three.' He turned to the other man.

'I'm assuming you're a doctor,'

'Dr Hall.' replied the man, putting his stethoscope into his bag. 'My practice is just opposite the station. One of the porters summoned me to tell me a man was injured on the train. But when I got there, well…it was too late.'

'Cause of death?' asked Ludd.

'Not for me to say definitively, but likely to be the knife wound to the chest, most likely to the heart. Death would have been more or less instantaneous, poor devil.'

'Right, thank you doctor, that will be all,' said Ludd. 'One of our doctors will deal with the rest. I expect there will need to be a post-mortem.'

The doctor hurried away, pleased to be relieved of any further official duties.

Ludd pushed through the small gaggle of onlookers on the main platform. He waved his warrant card at the constable on the platform gate who allowed him and McPherson to pass.

Ludd looked at the little group of people standing around the open door of the train carriage, sighed, and realised his half day off to dig over the flower beds in his garden would probably have to be cancelled.

Ludd and McPherson approached the carriage and looked into the compartment; the body had not been moved but had been covered with a railwayman's overcoat.

'Who put this on him?' asked Ludd to the small group, with irritation in his voice.

'I did,' said a uniformed railwayman.

'And you are…?'

'Bill Watkins, I'm the guard. It didn't seem right to leave Mr Cokeley there like that while we waited for you lot.'

'Well it *was* right to leave him there like that,' said Ludd. 'You've disturbed a crime scene.' He removed the coat gently and grimaced as he took in the man's glassy stare and the large patch of drying blood spread over his shirt-front and waistcoat.

'Here, you can have it back now,' Ludd said as he bundled up the coat and handed it to Watkins, who recoiled slightly at the touch of the fabric.

'Cokeley, you say?' asked Ludd to Watkins. 'Know him, did you?'

'Yes sir, Charles Cokeley, runs the antiques shop in Lower Addenham. I know him alright. But the woman that was with him…'

Ludd cut the man off. 'Yes, yes, we'll get to the rest of you in a minute.'

A dapper man with a colourful tie pushed forward to the compartment door. 'I say, chief, can we go now the cavalry's here? Some of us have got business deals to attend to.'

'And who are you?' asked Ludd. 'Rockefeller?'

The man did not share the joke. 'My name's Mr Symes and this is my business partner Mr Davis. We didn't see anything so you might as well let us go.'

There's always one, thought Ludd, as he turned to reply to the businessman. 'First of all, it's Inspector. I'm not a Chief – yet. And second, I've got a business to run as well, and that's finding out who did for this fellow before he does it to someone else. So be patient and I'll get to you in good time.'

Symes retreated back on to the platform and lit a cigarette, grumbling under his breath to Davis next to him.

'Knife wound to the chest, that's what the doctor said, wasn't it McPherson?' asked Ludd as he viewed the corpse.

'Right, sir.'

'Wrong, sergeant. Have another look and tell me why.'

McPherson stared down intently. 'I give up sir. It's a knife and it's in his chest. What's wrong about that?'

Ludd tutted. 'You fought in the war, didn't you?'

'No sir, I was still at school at the Armistice.'

Ludd muttered under his breath something about policemen getting younger all the time.

'Alright lad, fair enough. What's wrong is, that's not a knife, it's a bayonet.'

McPherson looked more closely. Ludd pointed to the handle of the weapon protruding from Cokeley's chest. 'See there, that's the clip that fixes it to the rifle. It's not one of ours though, I saw enough of those myself in the war. Looks like one of the old German ones.'

'Should we pull it out for a better look, sir?' asked McPherson, his voice taking on a slightly squeamish note.

'Certainly not,' replied Ludd. 'We'll leave that for the police doctor when he does his post-mortem.'

Ludd searched the man's pockets and pulled out a buff manila envelope.

'Hello, what's this...?' Ludd read from a letter typewritten on a thin sheet of paper.

'"Dear Mr Brown, we are pleased to confirm booking for double room for you and Mrs Brown on the 25th inst, and thank you for your advance of two pounds fifteen shillings, yours etc". Signed, general manager the Seaview Grand, Brighton. What do you make of that, McPherson?'

'Sounds like he was planning a dirty weekend with his girlfriend, sir'.

'You Scots like to put things bluntly, don't you?'

McPherson chuckled. 'Still, he had some imagination, at least he didn't call himself Smith'.

Ludd put the envelope in his pocket. 'I want to talk to the witnesses now, if we leave it any longer the trail's going to get as cold as this poor fellow here. We'll start with the guard.'

A few minutes later, Ludd and McPherson stood in the

guard's section of the carriage, holding tin mugs full of tea that had been prepared for them by the driver using some mysterious process of procuring boiling water from the engine. Before them stood Watkins, the guard, shifting his weight on his feet anxiously.

Ludd began asking questions while McPherson took notes. 'You're the one that found the body?'

'That's right,' replied Watkins, as he drew deeply on the stub of a cigarette. 'I thought Mr Cokeley had dropped off to sleep when I looked through the window. But then when I opened the door, I saw...well...I saw everything.'

'And nobody else was in the compartment?'

'That's what I was trying to tell you earlier. A woman, a blonde, she was, glamorous type, you know, got in with him at Lower Addenham, but I didn't see her get out. She can't have done, else I would have seen her when I was opening the doors.'

'She definitely got in his compartment?'

'I'm sure of it sir. And this is a non-vestibule carriage.'

'A non-what?'

'Non-vestibule, sir. No corridor between the compartments. Once you're shut in, you can't move about the train.'

'I see. But why were you keeping it free for Cokeley?'

'I always keeps a compartment free for Mr Cokeley, on account of him not liking to travel with anyone else on a Wednesday. He can't...he couldn't, be shut in with anyone on a Wednesday.'

'I've never heard of claustrophobia applying on certain days only.'

'Claustro...what's that you say, sir?'

'Never mind. What I'm trying to find out is, why did he want to travel alone? And if he did why did he let this mystery woman in?'

'I would have thought you lot knew all about it.'

'Kindly enlighten us, Mr Watkins,' sighed Ludd.

'Well,' responded the guard, 'he was robbed, see. A few years back. On the same line. On his own in a compartment with a feller who got on at Lower Addenham. Mr Cokeley always pays…paid in the takings from his shop to the bank here in Great Netley, and this chap robbed him on the way. Fair shook him up it did, and after that he used to slip me something to keep a compartment free for him every Wednesday.'

'So there's no bank in Lower Addenham then, I take it?'

'That's right sir. And it's always on a Wednesday he goes…went…because that's half day closing in Lower Addenham, so's he can leave the shop shut, but early closing here in Great Netley is a Thursday so the bank is open. It used to different here, mind, before the war, it was…'

Ludd cut the man off. 'Yes, yes, let's just stick to the matter in hand, shall we? So Cokeley was robbed a few years back, you say? Did they catch the fellow who did it?'

'I thought you fellows would know that,' replied Watkins in a confused tone. 'Yes, they caught him, he got five years I think, and that was getting off lightly if you ask me'.

'I'm not a walking encyclopaedia of crime,' replied Ludd. 'It was probably before my time so please do forgive me, won't you?' he added in a sarcastic tone.

'Now, let's carry on,' continued Ludd. 'Cokeley was robbed of the takings a few years ago. Shakes him up presumably so much he won't travel with anyone else in the compartment. I'm assuming he didn't have a car or a motor cycle?'

'Not Mr Cokeley, no,' replied Watkins. 'I said that to him after the business with the robbery. Ought to get yourself a motor car, I said, even though that was taking business away from the railway, like, I said then you'd be safe in that. "Not likely", he said, "too expensive, motor cars, and anyway what's to stop somebody jumping on the running board and robbing me on the way?" Well, I had no answer to that. "No, he said, "Once I'm in that compartment alone I know I'm alright". Poor devil.'

'But he was happy for you to allow a woman, such as this disappearing one we've been talking about, to get in with him?' said Ludd.

Watkins chuckled. 'Oh he didn't mind a lady travel companion. Had an eye for a pretty face, did Mr Cokeley, if you know what I mean. He felt safe with a woman in the compartment, I think – question is did she feel safe with him?' He gave a rasping laugh and lit another cigarette.

'Yes, thank you, we'll stick to the theories,' said Ludd. 'Now, you say Cokeley took the train to Netley to pay in the takings at the bank. Do you know if had the money with him this time?'

'I think he did, sir,' replied Watkins thoughtfully. 'Yes, he was carrying that little doctor's bag, you know, a brown leather one, that he always kept the money in'.

'We didn't see any bag in the compartment, sir,' said McPherson, looking up from his notebook.

'And you're sure he was carrying it?' asked Ludd.

'Sure as I'm seeing you now, sir,' replied the guard.

McPherson spoke again. 'So it looks like he was robbed again, but this time whoever did it made sure he wasn't around to tell the tale.'

'Perhaps...'replied Ludd uncertainly, then turned to Watkins again.

'This woman you say you let into his compartment. I'd hate to think a woman could do this, but let's say she did. Could she have got off the train at any time?'

'I shouldn't think so, sir,' replied Watkins. 'She goes a fair old lick nearly all of the way, does this train, and if a slip of a girl like that jumped out she'd most likely break her neck.'

'What about when the train stopped here at the end of the run? Could she have got off without being seen?'

'I don't see how she could have,' asserted Watkins. If she'd got out on the platform side I would have seen her, and if she managed to get out on the other side of the train, well it's just a brick wall the whole length of the station, she'd have been even more of a sight trying to climb up onto the platform in that tight dress she was wearing.'

Ludd glanced out of the window on the side of the train which was away from the platform. He opened the guard's door on that side, looking down at a drop of several feet into a narrow gap between the train and a moss-clad brick wall, decorated with brightly coloured posters for Oxo cubes, Fry's chocolate and Empire Wine. The gravel by the tracks did not seem to be disturbed and he was minded to agree with Watkins' assertion that anybody trying to flee in this manner would make themselves more conspicuous, not less.

Sighing, he turned back into the guard's van and pulled the door closed. 'Are you sure there isn't anywhere else on the route where she could have jumped out? Do you have to stop or slow down anywhere?'

A flash of inspiration crossed Watkins' face. 'I clean forgot. We did stop for the signal at the main line junction. And somebody did jump out. What with finding Mr Cokeley...like that...I must have got a bit muddled.'

Ludd frowned. 'If you're up in court as a witness to all this, as I suspect you will be, you can't say you're getting a bit muddled when you're being cross-examined. Now, try to think. The train stopped at a signal, and then what?'

'Then...'Watkins paused before continuing, 'then I was looking down the line waiting for the signal to change. I was here with the brake, see, waiting to let it off.'

He pointed to what looked to Ludd to be a large steering wheel attached to the floor of the carriage, on the left hand side facing the engine.

'I'd put the brake on when I realised the driver up the front was braking too. That's to give him a bit of extra stopping power. We don't always stop at that signal but there must have been a London train coming through the main line.'

'Alright, don't worry about the technical details for now,' said Ludd, aware that he had several more statements to take. 'The train stopped and you looked out down the line.'

'That's right, I looked out this window here,' said the guard, putting his head out of the window facing the platform, 'and I looked down the track to the signal. And I sees someone getting off. But that's the odd thing, sir, it wasn't a woman!'

Ludd and McPherson exchanged glances.

'Describe what you saw,' asked Ludd.

'Just the back of a man, running off into the undergrowth by the signal.'

'Can you describe him?' asked McPherson.

Watkins paused. 'Well...hard to say, I only saw him from behind. Young I'd say, by the speed he was moving.'

'What was he wearing?' said Ludd.

'Dark suit, big scarf, cap pulled down, just an ordinary looking feller really. I reckon he was just trying to avoid his fare, you get that sometimes, tramps and that, jumping off, I've known it to happen afore. 'Specially since the slump started.'

'Was he carrying anything?' asked the Inspector.

'He had a couple of bags of some kind, now that I think of it, but he dropped one of them.'

'A sack, or a bag?'

'I think he dropped a sack, but when he ran off it looked like he might be holding a bag as well.'

'Was it Cokeley's takings bag?' asked McPherson.

'Couldn't rightly say,' said Watkins scratching his ear. 'Might have been, I suppose.'

'What compartment did he get out of?'asked McPherson, not looking up from his notebook.

'I didn't see that, I only heard the door slam and when I looked out he was running off.'

A look of horror then crossed the guard's face. 'Hey, you don't think it could be that feller that did for Mr Cokeley do you?'

'I don't think anything at this point, Mr Watkins,' said Ludd. 'I'm just trying to ascertain some facts. Now, you're absolutely sure you didn't let this man into Cokeley's compartment?'

'No sir, I didn't. Only that woman I told you about.'

'Alright Mr Watkins, you've been very helpful,' said Ludd briskly. McPherson, let's speak to the others.'

'What about the train, sir?' said Watkins querulously. Only it's due back in Lower Addenham soon.'

'This train's not going anywhere, it's a crime scene,' said Ludd. 'Go and talk to the station master about it, see if you can get a replacement running from the other platform.'

'I don't know about that sir…' said Watkins doubtfully.

'I'm running a murder enquiry, not a train timetable,' said Ludd wearily. 'It's really no concern of mine if you tell him or not but this train isn't going anywhere until we've had a good look over it.'

Looking duly admonished, Watkins hurried from the guard's van to speak to the station master.

Once they were alone in the carriage Ludd turned to his junior officer.

'Well, what do you think, McPherson?'

'Sounds like a robbery gone wrong sir. It's happened to him before, and it could even be the same fellow again'.

'Hmm,' replied Ludd. 'Could be. I don't recall that case and since neither of us were working this patch at that time we don't know anything about it. Do some digging back at the station and see if you can get a name.'

'Right sir, and what about the woman?'

'The mystery blonde, you mean? Lord knows. My guess is she was probably in on the robbery and got off the train here without anybody noticing. See if there's anybody in the area fitting that description who pulls this kind of caper.'

'What kind of caper would that be, sir?'

'You're a grown man McPherson, you can work it out. A man who lives off what are politely known as immoral earnings, who gets one of his "employees" to make advances at a gentleman and then when said gentleman's got his guard down, he gets bashed on the head, or in this case, stabbed in the heart.'

'I see,' said McPherson. 'But Watkins said it was only Cokeley and the woman in the compartment.'

'Yes, but he also said the train stopped and he saw a man jump off. Who's to say he didn't jump *on* the train just before?'

'Aye…you could be right there.'

'I'm not saying I'm right or wrong about anything just now,' replied Ludd. 'I'm just looking at what we know so far. Now, you start finding out about that man that robbed Cokeley last time and any accomplices he might have had. And tell the men to start looking along the line for that sack and anything else they might find.'

'Right sir. I'll get back to Midchester right away and start looking through the files. Will you be alright to carry on here sir?'

'I can look after myself, thank you, sergeant. Take the Morris, I'll hitch a lift back with the uniformed lads.'

Ludd sighed as he watched McPherson walk briskly down the platform. This was proving to be a puzzler alright, but in his experience, a case that seemed complicated at first often turned out to be simple; like a tangled ball of wool you just had to tug gently at one or two threads with sufficient persistence and in time, the whole lot would unravel.

Chapter Four

Shaw, still waiting on the platform at Great Netley station, wondered if it would be indecorous to smoke with a corpse lying so close to him. He decided it would. Besides, there was Goggins with his bad lungs to consider right next to him.

As he put his pipe back into his pocket he tried to avoid glancing through the open door of the compartment in which Cokeley lay, uncovered, but it was difficult to avoid seeing him, particularly as a constable had told them under no account must they move away from the platform.

Both Shaw and Goggins had encountered death at close quarters before, but that had been abroad and in the febrile atmosphere of war; a violent death in the peace of the English countryside seemed somehow more shocking.

'Poor devil,' said Goggins, staring at the open compartment door. 'I know we had our differences but still, that's no way for a man to go.'

'Indeed,' murmured Shaw, saying after that a silent prayer for the deceased.

He looked up to see the two flashily dressed men who had boarded the train earlier approaching. The taller one stuck out his hand. 'We don't know each other, sirs, but

I'm Mr Symes and this is my partner Mr Davis. We run the estate agency in Lower Addenham.' Shaw shook hands with the men, but Goggins merely nodded curtly.

'Sorry to meet under such circumstances, eh?' said Davis. 'Shocking, just shocking, but good for business though, I must say.'

'Good for business...?' asked Shaw, puzzled.

'What my partner means to say is,' interjected Symes, 'that the firm of Symes and Davis land agents extends their deepest sympathies to all concerned at this difficult time'. He then led Davis away from Shaw and Goggins and the two men began talking in quiet tones. Shaw noticed that Symes appeared to be admonishing Davis.

The plain-clothes policeman that Shaw had noticed earlier then approached the small group of passengers.

'My name is Ludd, Inspector Ludd, of Midchester Criminal Investigation Department,' said the man. 'I appreciate you've been kept waiting so I'll just take brief statements for now and if I need to know more we'll arrange for you to come to the station.'

Ludd then looked closely at Shaw.

'I believe we've met before, sir,' he said to the clergyman.

'I'm afraid you have the advantage of me,' said Shaw with a slight smile.

'Yes, I've got it now,' continued Ludd. 'You're the parson over at Lower Addenham. Mr Short.'

'Shaw.'

'Ah yes. At...All Souls, isn't it?'

'All Saints,' corrected Shaw, wondering when he could have met the Inspector.

'That's right,' continued the policeman. 'You married my sister's boy a few months back. John and Gladys Renfrew. Lovely service it was, and not too long.'

Shaw smiled. 'Brevity is the soul of wit, Inspector; I recall the wedding but, regretfully, not our meeting.'

Ludd seemed a little disappointed. 'Well, never mind. I'll deal with you first if I may. Would you be so kind as to step into the guard's van?'

The two men stepped into the little cabin and Ludd turned a page in his notebook. 'Now sir, you were in the next compartment to the deceased, I understand.'

'That is correct'.

'Did you see or hear anything unusual on the train?'

'Only the man running into the undergrowth.'

'When was this?'

'When the train stopped at the signal. I heard a shout and looked out of the window, on this side'. Shaw, facing the front of the train, indicated the left hand window. 'I saw a figure running along the track. He then threw, or perhaps dropped, some sort of sack or bag into the undergrowth.'

'How was he dressed?'

'Oh…in a nondescript manner; a working man's clothes; a dark suit and cap'.

'Did you see his face?'

'Only for an instant and at that distance I could not make out any features, other than he was clean shaven.'

'Clean…shaven…' repeated the Inspector slowly as he wrote the words into his pad with the stub of an indelible pencil. 'And did you hear anything during the journey?'

'There is rather a lot of noise on that line, Inspector, although it sounded as if a conversation took place between Mr Cokeley and the woman in his compartment. By the way, I don't recall seeing her among the other passengers on the platform. What happened to her?'

'That's what I'd like to know, sir. Can you describe this woman?'

'Rather glamorous for Lower Addenham. More the sort of woman one sees on the film posters.'

'American, you mean?'

'American looking, Inspector. Blonde hair of the very lightest shade, and wearing a close fitting costume. I did not hear her speak, so could detect no accent. I have certainly never seen such a woman our little village before.'

'I see,' replied Ludd. 'And you didn't see her, or anyone else other than the man on the track, get on or off the train at any other time?'

Shaw paused, lost in thought for a moment. 'I must correct you, Inspector,' said Shaw. 'I did not see the man I described physically descend from the train. I heard a door slam and looked out to see him on the track, but did not actually see him get off'.

Ludd smiled. 'You'll make a good witness in court, sir, if it comes to that. I can tell you're observant'.

'A clergyman is trained to discern a certain pattern in what one might call the tapestry of life, Inspector. Observation of spiritual detail can often translate into observation of material detail.'

'You've lost me now,' said Ludd.

'My apologies, Inspector. I have a bad habit of philosophical musings, for which my wife often admonishes me.'

At the word 'wife', Ludd's expression became more intense. 'Did you know the deceased, sir?'

'Mr Cokeley was a fairly regular attender at All Saints, Inspector, but I did not know him particularly well.'

'A devout sort of man, was he?'

Shaw paused. 'As Queen Elizabeth the First said, Inspector, "I have no desire to make windows into men's souls"'.

Ludd frowned. 'You've lost me again, sir. What I mean is, how can I put this to a man of the cloth…was, did he get on well with his wife, or was he the sort of man to play away from home?'

Shaw smiled at the euphemism. 'Inspector, I was a military chaplain in France for most of the war. I think I have probably seen, or at least heard described in the most graphic terms, every sin of which man is capable. If you are asking me if Mr Cokeley was an adulterer, truthfully I do not know. Why, may I ask, is it relevant?'

'At this stage I don't know if it's relevant sir, I'm just following a line of enquiry.'

'Of course, it is not for me to pry,' said Shaw apologetically. 'For all you know, I myself could be the guilty party, perhaps climbing into the next compartment when the train was stopped.'

Ludd sighed. 'This country has changed a lot since the war, but the day I start suspecting vicars are clambering around trains to stab their parishioners to death is the day I hang up my truncheon and retire.'

'Thank you for your confidence,' replied Shaw. 'All I can say is that Mr Cokeley and his wife were known to argue from time to time. In fact I am sorry to say Mr Cokeley was unpopular with a number of people in the village.'

'Unpopular enough to be murdered by one of them?'

'Perhaps, but it is also possible that it was a simple case of robbery with violence. You will know, of course, that Mr Cokeley was robbed on the same train some years ago.'

Ludd cleared his throat. 'Yes, I've got someone looking into that. It's the most likely explanation. Possibly even the same perpetrator.'

Ludd put away his notebook. 'Yes, well you've been very helpful Mr Shaw. I'd better speak to the other passengers now. Who's the old fellow who was in the compartment next to you?'

'Albert Goggins. Another of my parishioners.'

'Know him well?'

'Not particularly; I see him infrequently at church but that is all.'

'Would he have any reason to want Cokeley dead?'

Shaw paused for a moment before speaking. 'It seems unlikely, but I did overhear a rather a heated argument between them this morning.'

'What about?'

'Mr Cokeley is an antiques dealer, and was offering what Mr Goggins believed to be too low a price for some articles he wished to sell. There was also bad blood between them as Cokeley was Goggins' landlord and was attempting to evict him.'

'I see. And those other two on the train. Shifty looking types, that look like brush salesmen. Know them?'

'Some sort of land agents, I believe. I have not met them before today'.

Just then a police constable looked into the guard's van, touching the brim of his helmet in a salute to the Inspector.

'Sorry to interrupt sir, only the police doctor would like a word with you.'

Ludd approached the door and turned to Shaw. 'That will be all, I think, sir. Let me know if you remember anything else, won't you?'

'There is one thing, Inspector,' said Shaw.

'Yes?'

'It occurs to me that somebody ought to inform Mrs Cokeley as soon as possible of her husband's death. As her parish priest, I feel it would better be me rather than an anonymous police officer.'

'Hmm,' said Ludd. 'You're probably right. Seeing as you know her. Let me speak to the doctor and then I'll arrange a car to drive you over.'

The two men stepped out of the guard's van onto the platform in time to see Cokeley's body, covered with a white sheet, being carried away on a stretcher by two constables. The police doctor, a balding man in a dishevelled tweed suit, stepped forward, holding an object wrapped in a large handkerchief.

'Good afternoon, Inspector Ludd. I think you ought to have a look at this.'

Ludd nodded, saying only 'doctor' in greeting.

The doctor opened the handkerchief to show the bloodstained bayonet that had ended Cokeley's life. He held the weapon up to the light gingerly using a corner of the handkerchief.

'I thought it best to extract it prior to the removal of the corpse. There's an inscription on it.'

Ludd squinted at the small letters engraved along the glistening blade. Before he read out the inscription, Shaw suddenly realised that he had seen the weapon before.

Ludd read the words out slowly. '"To Colour Sergeant Albert Goggins, Royal Suffolk Regiment, in grateful memory of his service. From His Pals. May 1900."'

Shaw looked at Goggins, who was watching the proceedings from a few feet away. The colour had drained from his face and his jaw had slackened.

'Well, Colour Sergeant Goggins,' said Ludd firmly. 'I think you've got some explaining to do'.

Chapter Five

Following a brief detour for Shaw to deliver a hurriedly written note to the Rector of Great Netley excusing his absence from the luncheon meeting, the black Wolseley Hornet police car sped along the road to Lower Addenham.

Shaw, alone in the back of the vehicle, looked at the flat black surface of the cap of the driver in front of him, and pondered the revelation of the inscribed bayonet.

It implicated Goggins, of course, who clearly disliked Cokeley; but sufficiently so to murder him? And if he had, how had he, an almost elderly man clearly not in the best physical condition, managed to enter a railway compartment without a corridor on a fast moving train, and then return to his place, without being seen? It was fantastical.

If that were possible, thought Shaw, it was also possible for me to do it. He realised that Goggins' box of antiques had been in his care for a period of time, perhaps making him a suspect.

He realised he was lucky to have the trust of the Inspector so soon in the investigation, and thought of Goggins, travelling in less salubrious transport, presumably to a cell in Midchester police station.

Shaw felt the car slowing down as it neared Lower Addenham; he looked out to see a young man trudging along the side of the road with his hands in his pockets, with a worried look on his face. Shaw realised it was the same young man he had seen cycling past the vicarage in the morning; what was his name? He wracked his brains but could not recall it.

The police car stopped in the little square in the centre of Lower Addenham, and the driver turned round briefly to face Shaw.

'Is this the place, sir?'

'Yes, thank you constable,' said the clergyman. 'This will do.'

Shaw stepped out of the car, which sped away in the direction of Great Netley, presumably required for the myriad duties surrounding the murder investigation. He looked at the front of Cokeley's shop, with its drawn blinds and 'CLOSED' sign on the door.

Shaw remembered it was early closing day; he tried the handle but the door was locked so he knocked tentatively, then with greater force when no reply came. He was anxious to break the news to Mrs Cokeley before she heard it from some neighbour, or worse, read about in the evening newspapers.

He heard the rattle of a sash window being raised and the sound of dance music from a wireless drifting out.

A woman shouted from the window. 'Can't you read? We're closed.'

Shaw looked up to see Mrs Cokeley leaning out of the window, her bright blonde hair almost transparent in the sunshine. 'Oh, it's you, vicar,' she said. 'If it's about the church flower rota, I've told them I can't do this week.'

'No it's not about that, Mrs Cokeley', said Shaw. 'May I come in?'

51

'Alright then, I'll come down,' she replied, sounding slightly put out. 'Only I can't spare too long, mind, because Tommy Handley's on the Light Programme.'

A few minutes later, Mrs Cokeley was seated at her floral sofa in the little upstairs sitting room, dabbing the tears away from her heavily made-up eyes with a small lace handkerchief. She then blew her nose noisily.

'I just can't believe it, vicar. My Charlie, dead…murdered! I mean, who would do such a thing?'

Mrs Cokeley's apparent grief was somewhat at odds, thought Shaw, with the jolly dance-band music coming from the large wireless set in the corner.

'Who indeed?' answered Shaw. 'Rest assured the police are doing all they can to catch the person who did this.'

'Well I hope they do catch him!' exclaimed Mrs Cokeley angrily. 'I suppose whoever it was took his money as well.'

Mrs Cokeley must have noticed Shaw's slightly raised eyebrow, as she then added 'I mean…well, I'm a widow now, aren't I? I'll have to watch every penny from now on. I've got no children and well, that life insurance policy he had isn't likely to keep me very well'.

'Have faith, Mrs Cokeley,' said Shaw. 'After all, you have a business which brings in money, which is something to be thankful for.'

'This place?' said Mrs Cokeley with a bitter laugh. 'We don't make much here, a couple of pounds a week at best, and I'm not taking up shop work at my time of life. There's barely enough to cover Miss Ellis's wages.'

'Miss Ellis?'

'The shop assistant. And she's not much help. She asked

to go home early today even before Charlie closed up, said her mother was ill and she had to look after her. I had to close the whole place because I wasn't going to miss Billy Cotton, well I can't hear the wireless down here in the shop and I shouldn't have to move it, should I?'

'Er, quite, Mrs Cokeley,' said Shaw, standing up. 'I shall not intrude any longer. Rest assured I will do everything in my power to help you. I will call again regarding funeral arrangements. Perhaps, before I go...a moment of prayer?'

'That's very kind but I don't think I've got time, vicar,' said Mrs Cokely, glancing down at her open copy of *Radio Times* and popping a chocolate in her mouth. 'Henry Hall's on in a minute'.

The news of the murder created a sensation in Lower Addenham that evening, unlike anything since the outbreak of war on that hot August day in 1914, when straw-hatted men had pushed and shoved each other at the railway station, desperate to secure the late editions of the newspapers. Now, as then, the rumours spread like a forest fire as neighbour spoke gossip unto neighbour.

Nobody could remember the last time there had been a murder in the village; in the public houses the white-haired oracles were consulted; some thought it had been in '78, others claimed it was still further back, in '54.

One wizened sage, very deaf, was confused and believed that war had broken out again. 'Is it the Huns or the Frogs this time?' he enquired, and was puzzled by the roar of laughter this produced in his fellow drinkers.

Speculation on the morals of Mr Cokeley and Mr

Goggins was rife; an enterprising small businessman acquainted with the racing fraternity even opened a book on the matter, with highly favourable odds on Goggins' guilt.

In the more genteel parlours and comfortable drawing rooms of the village, there were whispers of such sins as adultery and tax evasion in the Cokeley household, and of murderous desire for revenge by Mr Goggins, brought on by some ancient feud between the two men over the love of a young woman in the reign of Queen Victoria.

The crime happened too late for the local newspapers, but those with wireless sets heard a brief mention of the incident on the BBC's nine o'clock new bulletin, and they were thrilled to hear the name of their little village announced to the nation. Finally the last lights were extinguished, and the villagers went to sleep, eager with anticipation of the morning newspapers.

The following day, the weather was bright and sunny again but this time, Shaw sat at the breakfast table devoid of the previous day's feeling of contentment. After a troubled night he had risen earlier than usual, hoping that breakfast would make him feel better.

Was it contentment he had felt yesterday, or complacency? he wondered. A text sprang into his mind: What was it? Revelations? No, Thessalonians, chapter five, verse two. 'For you yourselves know perfectly that the day of the Lord so comes as a thief in the night.' One must always be ready for the unexpected, he thought, even for such things as a murdering thief in a railway carriage.

'Come back, Lucian dear,' said his wife with a smile, as

she poured him a cup of English Breakfast tea. 'You're lost in thought again. Is it this awful business about poor Mr Cokeley?'

Shaw raised his cup and saucer to drink his tea, with a distracted expression.

'I'm sorry, Marion, you were saying?'

'The murder. It's perfectly ghastly. I've been reading all about it in the *Gazette*.' She pointed to the regional daily newspaper propped up on the table, the front page of which featured a grainy photograph of Cokeley accompanied by the headline: *Grisly Murder of Antiques Dealer.*

'It says here he was stabbed fifteen times,' said Mrs Shaw, taking another bite of her toast and marmalade, 'and that the railway compartment was quite dripping with blood.'

'Nonsense,' said Shaw in an annoyed tone. 'I do wish these muckrakers would stop making things up.'

He turned to his own newspaper, the *Church Times*, and tried to read a rather less sensational article on the use of the Eastward Position during Holy Communion.

After a few minutes he could no longer concentrate and put the newspaper down, turning to his wife to muse aloud.

'I feel I ought to help in some way.'

'With what, dear?'

'With the investigation.'

'But you're not a policeman, dear.'

'No, but I am the vicar of this parish and therefore have a responsibility for the well-being of its inhabitants, particularly Mr Goggins.'

Mrs Shaw smiled. 'You are a very diligent parson, dear. How did Chaucer put it?' She thought for a moment. 'Oh yes. "A good man was ther of religioun". But that doesn't make you a detective.'

'I do not intend to be one, my dear. But I may be able to provide some assistance to the police, that they otherwise would not have.'

'Such as what?'

'I can, perhaps, use my position to glean information that they are not privy to.'

Mrs Shaw finished the last of her toast. 'You're being obtuse again, dear. Anyway, you said you're going to meet the organist today about the repairs to the pipes, so you won't have time to be an amateur sleuth.'

'I'm going out for a walk instead,' said Shaw, amused by the puzzled expression on his wife's face.

At the sound of the word 'walk', Fraser jumped up from under the table and looked up at his master with an adoring expression.

'Come along, Fraser,' said Shaw. 'I will drop in on Laithwaite on the way. He can tend to the problems of the organ. It will be good practice for him.'

As Shaw stood in the hallway putting the lead on Fraser, his wife looked at him with mock annoyance.

'I say, you're not going to become like one of those Victorian clerics, are you? Getting their poor curates to do everything while you go off collecting butterflies or something?'

'Certainly not, my dear,' said Shaw, putting on his hat. 'I intend to collect something – or someone – far more important than a butterfly.'

Mrs Shaw shook her head in disbelief as she watched her husband stride down the garden path, flourishing his walking stick, while Fraser trotted along at his heel, his little white tail wagging furiously.

Shaw walked along the dirt road that led from Lower Addenham to Great Netley, which ran parallel for most of the way with the little branch railway line.

After a couple of miles he noticed several police constables, walking slowly along the line towards him; they carried long staves and were prodding the undergrowth by the side of the track.

He heard one of the men call out. 'Keep going lads, we're about halfway there now. Let me know the moment you see anything.'

Shaw, unnoticed by the constables, continued with his walk. Fraser, despite his short legs, seemed never to tire on long walks and maintained his enthusiasm throughout.

A mile or so further on, Shaw saw the red and white painted signal arm by the side of the track, outlined starkly against the sky. He paused; there were faint tracks of what was perhaps a motorcycle or bicycle on the dirt road, visible for just a few feet before they faded into the mud.

The grass and weeds between the road and the railway track seemed to have been disturbed in a line; this must have been the point where the unidentified man ran from the railway to the road.

But something was not right. He squatted and looked again, and realised the grass had been disturbed in *two* lines. Standing up, he thought, yes; that was it; the angle of the flattened grass suggested someone had walked, or run, onto the railway and then back off again on to the road, perhaps to depart by motorcycle. But the trail leading on to the railway led directly to the signal.

Shaw walked to the railway track, keeping his distance from the trails in the grass so as not to disturb them.

As with all English railway lines, a protective wire fence had been built alongside to prevent livestock straying into danger. The line of disturbed grass ended in a clump of bushes near the signal. Shaw prodded the nearest fence post with his stick. The post wobbled and two of the lengths of wire connected to it sagged and fell to the ground, leaving a gap large enough, Shaw realised, for a man to climb through.

Not wishing to trespass, Shaw examined the signal on the other side of the fence. It was mounted on a wooden platform, chipped and scratched on the side nearest him. Dense shrubbery and high weeds surrounded its base.

Looking down at the railway line, he could see that some of the tall weeds by the signal had been disturbed, perhaps by the boots of the policemen who had just passed that way.

He wondered whether they too had noticed the tracks in the grass between the signal and the road; surely they must have? But when he looked back, through some trick of the light, these were not visible.

He realised that Fraser was no longer at his feet, and looked around for the little dog. There was no sign of him, so he called out his name sharply. Instantly, there came an excited barking in response, from a patch of undergrowth further along the track. Fraser was alternatively yelping and pulling at an object in the bushes.

'What is it, boy, what have you found?' asked Shaw excitedly.

Fraser soon dragged a sack from under a clump of weeds; Shaw recalled the man leaving the train had thrown or dropped something here; perhaps that was it? Consumed with curiosity, but thinking it was probably just some track-side refuse, Shaw prodded the opening of the sack and recoiled as a shock of peroxide blonde hair tumbled out.

'Get back, Fraser, heel,' he commanded, and the dog stood back obediently, his stubby tail wagging excitedly.

Shaw crouched down and, with a certain hesitation, gingerly opened the bag and looked inside. Inside was a blonde wig, some sort of dress and a pair of women's high-heeled shoes. Close by, the fence sagged again where, Shaw surmised, somebody had climbed over to make the tracks on the grass back to the road.

Shaw thought for a moment. The policemen who had passed earlier had, presumably, missed this piece of evidence, which would have been invisible to anyone cursorily inspecting the sides of the track. He decided the best course of action was to walk back to Lower Addenham with the peculiar findings and present them to to the police.

Chapter Six

'We can't keep him much longer sir,' said McPherson to Ludd, as the pair sat down in the interview room deep within the bowels of Midchester police station. The morning sun shone weakly through the barred window high up in white-painted brick wall, illuminating the blue plume of smoke rising from McPherson's first cigarette of the day.

'You're right that we haven't got much to go on,' said Ludd, 'but until any news comes in of that fellow who robbed Cokeley five years back, then Goggins is the best we have to go on. We'll give him one more try this morning to see what we can find out, and if we can't charge him, we'll let him go. By the way, *has* any news come in of…what did you say his name was?'

'West, sir, Reginald West,' said McPherson, consulting his notebook. 'Convicted for robbery, did four years hard labour in Parkhurst then got transferred to Ipswich gaol for the last year of his sentence. Let out four weeks ago. I managed to get through on the telephone to his probation officer just this morning; he's having some trouble finding an address for him but he's promised to call me back.'

'Trouble finding an address?' snorted Ludd. 'Doesn't surprise me. Do-gooders, most of these probation officers, and most couldn't find their you-know-what with both hands tied behind their back. Anyway, good work – let me know as soon as he gives you an address, and we'll lift this West chap.'

'Right sir,' smiled McPherson. 'Shall I get Goggins sent in here now?'

'Yes, go on. He should have finished his breakfast by now. Maybe he'll be in more of a mood to talk.'

McPherson grimaced and asked the constable outside to fetch Goggins from his cell.

A few moments later, the elderly saddler walked awkwardly into the room, his suit rumpled from being slept in and his shirt collar and tie absent. He sat down at the scarred table facing Ludd and McPherson.

'Good morning Mr Goggins, I trust you slept well?' Ludd offered the man a Wills Gold Flake cigarette from the packet on the table.

Goggins shook his head and pushed the packet away. 'Can't complain.'

'Feeling a bit more like talking today?' added McPherson.

'You mean, do I feel like admitting to murdering Cokeley? If that's what you mean then no. I was in a Boer camp for six weeks and those blighters never broke me so I'm not worried about you lot.'

'Yes, we've had a look into your record in the South African War,' said Ludd. 'Chum of mine in the War Office read it out to me over the telephone yesterday evening. Quite impressive, I must say.'

'What's that got to do with anything? That was thirty year ago,' grumbled Goggins.

Ludd consulted his notebook. 'According to the official record, you led a break out from a Boer prison camp on 27th April 1900 by overpowering a guard and killing him with his own bayonet, enabling you and six comrades to escape to the British lines. You were something of a hero, I'd say.'

Goggins looked at the floor. 'Say what you like. I did my duty and that's all there was to it.'

'Exhibit A,' said Ludd, opening a brown envelope beside him and removing the bayonet, lately taken from Cokeley's body. He placed it on the table and pushed it towards Goggins.

'One Mauser bayonet, 1895 pattern. Inscribed on the blade with the following words, "To Colour Sergeant Albert Goggins, Royal Suffolk Regiment, in grateful memory of his service. From His Pals. May 1900." Yours, I take it?'

'Of course it's mine,' said Goggins.

'Just one thing, for the record, sir,' said McPherson. 'Why's it a German bayonet? The Boer War wasn't anything to do with Germany.'

Ludd opened his mouth to speak but Goggins interrupted.

'The Boers weren't soldiers, they were Dutch settlers, just a bunch of farmers. Had all kinds of weapons, whatever they could get. They liked the Mauser because it was accurate and they could pick us off like blasted crows on a farmer's field'.

'Why did your fellow soldiers engrave the thing for you?' asked Ludd.

'Thankful, I suppose. Took us two days to reach the British lines and that was the only weapon we had between us apart from sticks and stones. I used it to kill a few pheasants for us to eat. Ever tried raw pheasant?'

McPherson swallowed uncomfortably, the taste of his breakfast porridge still in his mouth.

'So I suppose it was symbolic, like, that bayonet,'

continued Goggins. 'When we got to Bloemfontein and got set up again with the regiment, it went missing from my billet. I reckoned someone must have stolen it, but a few days later the lads did a little presentation of it, all polished up and with that engraving on it they'd got done in a jeweller's shop in the town.'

'How did you kill him?' said Ludd abruptly.

There was a pause and then Goggins replied. 'Kill who?'

Ludd frowned. 'The guard in the Boer prison camp.'

Goggins looked Ludd in the eye and spoke slowly. 'I stabbed him through the heart.'

'Interesting,' said the Inspector. 'That's just how Cokeley was killed.'

Goggins swallowed. 'Well I didn't have anything to do with it.'

'We've heard there was a bit of bad feeling between you and Mr Cokeley, is that right?' asked McPherson.

'Who told you that?'

Ludd leaned forward. 'Never you mind. What I want to know is, if you had nothing to do with it, who was it who used your little souvenir on Cokeley?'

'It could have been anybody,' said Goggins. I left it with a whole lot of other stuff for valuation in his shop. Anybody in there could have took it.'

'What if we told you we found your fingerprints on it?' asked McPherson.

'What if you did?' replied Goggins angrily. 'That don't prove anything.'

'It so happens we didn't find any prints on it, Mr Goggins,' interjected Ludd. 'Whoever did for Cokeley was careful and probably wore gloves or wiped everything, as we didn't find any prints on the door handle of the train compartment either.'

McPherson looked at his watch and lit another cigarette.

He leaned forward and pointed the smouldering tip at Goggins, who coughed.

'Here's what I think happened,' said the Scotsman. 'I think you paid some tart to keep Cokeley distracted in that compartment, and at some point during the train journey you climbed out of your compartment along the outside of the train, got into Cokeley's, stabbed him and took his money. Tossed it somewhere along the line to pick up later, then got back in to your own compartment.'

'Rubbish,' snorted Goggins. 'Climbing along moving trains? Who do you think I am, Buster Keaton? And what are you on about paying some tart?'

McPherson leaned forward. 'An attractive blonde woman was seen getting into Cokeley's compartment but when the train arrived at Great Netley, there was no sign of her. I reckon you and her could have been in it together.'

Goggins simply shook his head in disbelief.

Ludd sighed. 'I'll admit my sergeant has something of a fertile imagination,' he said, 'but theoretically it's possible. We're trying to eliminate you from our enquiries.'

'I'll help you then,' said Goggins. 'I'm 62 years old. My lungs is packed up and I've got a bad arm. That train gets up to 30 or 40 miles per hour and sways about like a drunken sailor. If you think I could manage what you say, good luck proving it.'

McPherson seemed annoyed. 'We can always get a doctor to examine you.'

'Well why don't you, then? And while he's here he can examine this!' Goggins grabbed the bayonet and before McPherson or Ludd could stop him, he plunged the blade into his tweed-clad right leg.

Both the detectives inhaled sharply, expecting a surge of blood from a horrific injury; but none came.

Goggins smiled and rapped the side of his leg with his knuckles, looking up with an amused expression at the two amazed policemen. 'That's another little war souvenir I got. Cork leg. So if you think a man with one leg can clamber about a moving train, good luck to yer, but I reckon any judge would laugh that out of court.'

After Goggins had been released and sent home (in a squad car summoned by a somewhat guilty-feeling Inspector Ludd), the two detectives sat drinking tea at their desks in Midchester police station.

'Look, McPherson,' said the Inspector, dipping a biscuit into his tea, 'I know you Scots are a romantic lot but try to keep the fantasies under control. It looks unprofessional.'

'Fantasies, sir?' replied McPherson.

'That stuff about Goggins climbing about a moving train like Harold Lloyd.'

'It's no' a fantasy sir. Alright, Goggins probably could'nae do it, but somebody could. It's a possibility.'

'So's Ipswich Town winning the Football Association Cup, but it's not blooming likely, is it?'

'I wouldn't know sir. I follow Partick Thistle myself. If Goggins didn't do it, who did?'

'I'm not ruling out Goggins just yet,' replied Ludd. 'But we haven't got enough to go on to keep him here. My money's on this being a double act with that mystery blonde and whoever it was jumped off the train.'

The telephone on Ludd's desk rang and he answered it with his name then listened in silence. After a few moments he replied.

'Yes, keep him there, I'd like a word with him.'

After replacing the receiver, he swallowed the last of his tea quickly and strode to the row of pegs by the door to put on his hat and raincoat.

'That was one of the lads searching the line at Lower Addenham,' said Ludd. 'Seems that vicar's found something interesting and that I ought to have a look.'

'Vicar?' said McPherson, with a puzzled expression.

'Don't look so ignorant,' replied Ludd. 'They call them ministers in your part of the world.'

'I know what a vicar is sir, but what's he got to do with us?'

'He was on the train. Not a suspect, if I know my job, but he knows the local area and people and I think he could be useful. I'll get on to it while you keep on trying to track down West.'

Just then the telephone on McPherson's desk rang. He put down his cup and saucer and lifted the receiver. 'Detective Sergeant McPherson,' he said quickly. 'Yes, good, what's the address?'

He began to scribble quickly on his pad with an indelible pencil. After the call was ended, he turned to Ludd with a smile. 'That was the probation officer. They've got an address for West.'

'Right,' said Ludd, jamming his bowler hat onto his head. 'You pick him up while I speak to this vicar. Take a couple of lads with you, he could cut up rough.'

'Should we draw arms, sir?' answered McPherson enthusiastically.

'Where do you think we are, Chicago?' said Ludd, raising his eyebrows. 'Just pick him up and be careful about it. If he is our killer he might not worry too much about doing it again.'

McPherson grabbed his hat and coat and the two men walked rapidly down the stairs towards the motor pool.

Chapter Seven

In the site office of Symes and Davis, Symes was showing a young couple one of the company's glossy brochures.

'And this, sir, is the *piece de resistance* (he pronounced it in the English way) of the whole blooming lot: the Hollywood Mexican Moderne Villa,' said Symes, smoothing the brochure out on his desk. 'Four bedrooms, two reception rooms, bathroom, downstairs cloakroom, garage, finished in Alpine White stucco with tiled roof and detailing in Acapulco Green.'

The young couple looked at each other doubtfully.

'What's Acapulco?' asked the man. 'Is that like asbestos?'

Symes paused before replying. He wasn't quite sure what Acapulco was either.

'It's the very latest in roofing, that's for sure,' he said brightly.

The man twirled his hat in his hands. 'It's a little pricey, especially for something a long way from the station.'

Symes shrugged. 'There's a lot of demand for this type of property nowadays. The housing market's booming, prices will only be going up, so it's best to buy now.'

The young man frowned. 'But we're in a slump. Worst slump ever, the papers are saying. How can house prices be going up?'

'Economics, sir, economics,' said Symes, blandly. 'If I were to explain it all to you, by the time I'd finished the prices would have gone up even more, so, what say we put your name down for this lovely residence? Nothing to pay until September. Plenty of time to change your minds.' He held out a fountain pen.

'We'll have a think about it,' said the man. 'I need to be getting back to the office,' he added, and stood up. 'Come along, Muriel,' he said to his wife.

'What is there to think about?' said Symes, beginning to lose patience. 'There's a queue of people a mile long waiting to move into places like this.'

The man walked to the door, his wife following meekly. 'As I said, we'll think about it and let you know. Good day.'

'Wait a minute, you haven't looked at the Anne Hathaway Jacobethan De Luxe yet...'

Symes was cut off in mid-patter by the slamming of the office door as the potential customers left.

'Well done Symesie, another unsatisfied customer,' chuckled Davis, who had been sitting at his desk smoking and idly admiring the figure of Miss Frobisher, who as usual was sitting at the reception desk polishing her nails.

'I can't understand it,' said Davis. 'What is it with these people? They've got the chance to live in the home of their dreams for only fifty quid down, and they're not interested.'

'Maybe they've got tight-fisted employers, and haven't got fifty quid to spare,' said Miss Frobisher dryly, while she filed down a particularly tough bit of fingernail.

Symes bridled at this remark. 'You don't exactly have onerous duties here so I think we pay you enough.'

'Oh I don't mind the pay,' said Miss Frobisher archly.

'it's the extra-curricular duties I'm expected to carry out that I object to.'

Davis looked over at Symes, whose face was flushed with embarrassment. 'Extra-cu-what? What's she on about?'

'Never you mind,' said Symes decisively, clapping his hands together then rubbing them. 'Let's not be downhearted. Now that Cokeley's gone we can get that access road built, and the sales will start rolling in.'

'Cokeley?' asked Miss Frobisher. 'That poor old chap who got killed on the train yesterday? I don't think that's anything to celebrate. Ooh, gives me the creeps,' she said with a shudder.

'His wife's bound to sell up now,' continued Symes enthusiastically. 'Well, stands to reason, she'll need the money, won't she? I told you the problem would get solved one way or another. How about we do a press release to the local paper announcing the new access road?'

Davis looked at Symes and Miss Frobisher and frowned. 'Steady on Symsie. We don't want to go spreading it around that we had something to gain from old Cokeley snuffing it.'

'Why not?' queried Symes.

'Well...people might think...'

'Might think what?'

'Never mind.'

'Right,' said Symes, shaking his head as if to rid his brain of Davis' interruption, 'as I was saying, we'll put something in the local rag about the new road, and watch if the till doesn't start ringing soon. Take a letter please, Ruth.'

Miss Frobisher sighed, put down her nail file and picked up her shorthand pad.

The constable emerged from the little ticket office at Lower Addenham station where he had been speaking on the telephone. He approached Shaw, who was standing in the station forecourt.

'The Inspector's on his way sir. If you wouldn't mind waiting for a bit, he says he'd like to talk to you about what you found.'

'Very well,' replied the clergyman. 'I shall wait here at the station for him.'

The policeman went over to join his colleague on the little station driveway where they were keeping back a small group of mackintosh-clad reporters hoping for an exclusive on the murder. Shaw noticed they looked extremely bored, probably from the lack of newsworthy activity.

Shaw walked into the station and sat down on one of the dark green benches in the ticket hall. He filled a pipe and lit it, while Fraser snuggled down under the bench with a contented sigh. Shaw puffed on his pipe, enjoying the aroma and looking at the brightly coloured posters on the walls advertising excursions to holiday resorts and historic cities; Lowestoft, York, Durham. His eye then caught the timetable and he noticed the section marked 'connections to London mainline trains via Great Netley.'

Something stirred in Shaw's memory. London mainline trains, he read again. Something about yesterday's events; what was it? He decided the best way to jog his memory might be simply to think about something else.

He noticed Watkins, the guard, idling on the platform by the little shuttle train which was presumably waiting to depart on its next journey. He was talking to a squat man with a soot stained face, small round spectacles and soiled clothing, which was black except for a bright red neckerchief around his neck. Shaw recognised him as the train driver, having noticed him waiting along with the other witnesses to be interviewed by the police at Great Netley the previous day. Watkins noticed Shaw and walked over.

'Morning, vicar,' he said, touching the peak of his cap. 'Terrible old do yesterday, weren't it?'

'Indeed,' replied Shaw, standing up and walking towards Watkins, with Fraser trotting behind on his lead.

'I was just saying that to Perce here,' continued Watkins. Terrible old do, wasn't it, Perce?'

'You was, Bill,' replied the driver. 'Never seen the like of it. A murder round here, well it's shocking. And not much shocks me vicar, I'm from the big city originally, you see.'

'London?' asked Shaw.

'No, Yarmouth,' replied the driver with a chuckle. 'Get all sorts happening there,' said the driver. 'But you don't expect anything like that here.' He shook his head in disbelief.

'By the way vicar,' he added, 'I don't believe we've met. Percy Ambler.' He quickly inspected his right hand, wiped it deftly on his trousers and offered it to Shaw.

'How do you do,' said Shaw, ignoring the sensation of a grimy residue on his fingers.

'Catching the next train are you, sir?' asked Watkins. 'They've given us a new carriage, same as the old one, but they've kept the other at the sidings up at Netley as they're still poking around on it.'

'No,' replied Shaw. 'I'm waiting to see the Inspector who is investigating the case.'

'Ah,' replied Percy. 'Well if you'll excuse me sir, I've got to be getting up steam for the next run, so I'll leave you two be.'

'Righto Perce,' said Watkins. 'I'll be in the guard's van getting a brew on. They've got a fancy new electric stove in that new carriage, and I've got to work out how to use it.' He walked off down the platform.

Shaw was suddenly inspired to ask something. 'I wonder if, Mr Ambler, you might allow me to have a quick look at the cab. Engines have always been of interest to me.'

Ambler beamed. 'Certainly vicar, step right up. She's a beautiful old girl, this one,' he said, patting the side of the engine. 'The Holmes J83,' he added. 'But we likes to call her Nelly. Don't ask me why.'

Shaw tied Fraser's lead to a post on the platform, and climbed into the little cab with its smell of coal dust, oil and hot metal. There were two forward facing windows, rather like portholes, one on the left and one on the right, through which Shaw could see the single track stretching out ahead to Great Netley.

Another black-clad man was inside, much younger than Ambler. 'This here's our fireman, George. George, the vicar's come to have a look around.'

'Oh right sir,' said the stoker, and held out his hand to Shaw. 'George Webb, pleased to meet yer.'

The two men shook hands and once again Shaw had the sensation of an oily residue on his palms.

'It may seem a strange question, Mr Ambler,' said Shaw cautiously, 'but did you at any time see a woman climb off the train yesterday?'

Ambler and Webb exchanged smiles. 'Ah,' said the driver, 'you mean the vanishing lady. Bill told me all about that. Said she looked like a film star. Personally I think he imagined it. Been cooped up in that guard's van of his too long, he has.'

'I fear he did not imagine it,' said Shaw. 'I also saw a woman get on the train, though I did not see her face.'

'I'm only joking, vicar,' said Ambler, his eyes glinting from behind the small round lenses of his spectacles. 'If Bill says he saw her, then he saw her. What I don't understand is how she got *off* the train.'

A thought struck Shaw. 'Could she perhaps have concealed herself in some way on the train?'

'Not likely,' said Ambler. 'There's only the space under the seats, and that would be obvious to anyone. There's nowhere else to hide in those carriages.'

'Perhaps she jumped off?' enquired Shaw.

'Not likely neither,' continued the driver. 'Anyone jumping off this train when she's rattling along would likely break their neck, especially a slip of a girl like Bill said he saw.'

Webb interjected. 'The only time she might have got off was when we stopped for the signal and you said that lad jumped off.'

'I've thought of that,' said Ambler. 'The police took a statement from me yesterday but they didn't seem that intcrested. Last night I was thinking over what happened a bit more. The only person I saw jump off the train was that lad that Bill saw. If a woman had jumped off we'd have noticed that, I reckon.'

'Yes, I noticed the man running away,' said Shaw. 'Presumably if anyone else had done so, at least one of you or the guard would have seen him or her.'

'Well in all honesty I didn't see this fellow nor anyone else,' said Webb. 'Most of the time I was stoking the boiler making sure we had enough steam. I heard Perce here shout out though.'

'I saw him alright, even if you didn't,' said Ambler. 'I

had my hand on the regulator and I looked out to see a young chap dash across the field.'

'Forgive my ignorance,' said Shaw. 'But what is the regulator?'

'That's this 'ere,' said Ambler, patting a large red lever on the right side of the cab. 'In layman's terms, this controls the speed of the train, like the what do you call it, the accelerator, on a motor car,' he added. 'I was looking out of my window, waiting for the signal to change then I heard a door slam somewhere behind, and I sees that young chap racing off.'

'Which is your window?' asked Shaw.

'This one on the right,' said Ambler. 'So I heard a shout, turns round to look behind and there he is, running off back the way we come.'

'And you didn't think to give chase?' enquired Shaw.

'Chase the blighter? Not likely. Not worth me risking my neck over a tuppenny fare. I didn't know he'd killed someone.'

'If I'd seen him on my side I'd've whacked the bugger with my shovel,' said Webb. ''scuse my French, vicar,' he added apologetically.

Shaw smiled. 'A rather unreasonable use of force to detain a fare-dodger, I would have thought.'

'How's that, vicar?' asked Webb.

'At the time nobody knew a murder had been committed on the train.'

'Ah right, I see,' said Webb. 'And of course we don't know whoever that was that ran off was the killer anyway.'

'Come off it George, who else would it be?' said Ambler. 'No, once they catch whoever that chap was, that's your killer right there.'

'I certainly hope so,' replied Shaw.

'Well if you don't mind, vicar,' said Ambler, consulting the fob watch chained to his waistcoat. 'We're off in a few minutes, so we'd best get organised.'

'Of course,' said Shaw, 'Thank you so much for showing me the cab. A boyhood ambition realised. Oh, there is one more thing that interests me.'

'Yes, vicar?' asked Ambler. 'I'm always glad to help a railway enthusiast.'

'Who controls the signal on the line from here to Great Netley?'

'Well now,' said Ambler hesitantly. 'There's only the one signal, before the main line junction, so that would be controlled from the box at Great Netley.'

'Visiting a signal box has always been an ambition of mine also,' said Shaw.

'Why don't you have a look one day?' replied Ambler. Old Bert Fox works that box. He's a pal of mine, tell him I sent you, he'll be happy to show you around.'

Shaw thanked the men and stepped down from the cab. He turned to face the bulky form of Inspector Ludd.

'Thinking of a career change, Mr Shaw?' said the Inspector laconically.

'Good morning, Inspector. The driver and fireman were kind enough to show me the cab while I was waiting here for you.'

'I'm not much keen on trains myself,' replied Ludd. 'Waste of time hanging around for them. Give me a fast motor-car any day. That's the future, you mark my words.'

'Perhaps,' replied Shaw with an indulgent smile. 'Tell me, how is Mr Goggins?'

'We've let him go,' said Ludd.

'Is he no longer a suspect?'

Shaw untied Fraser from his post, allowing the little dog to jump up into his arms. He patted him briefly then placed him gently on the platform.

'I haven't ruled anything or anyone out yet,' said Ludd. 'But we got the police doctor to look him over and I doubt he's capable of climbing a long flight of stairs, let alone clambering all over a moving train.'

'That is most interesting, Inspector,' said Shaw. 'May I also enquire, as to the release of Mr Cokeley's body? As his parish priest it will fall to me to officiate at his funeral, and I am anxious to begin arrangements.'

Ludd nodded and looked around the platform briefly. 'I've had confirmation from the police doctor that Cokeley died from the wound to his heart. We'll need Mrs Cokeley to come in and formally identify the body and then once the coroner's made a decision, we'll be releasing his body.'

'Thank you for letting me know,' said Shaw. 'I shall visit Mrs Cokeley today to inform her.'

Shaw noticed that Ludd was holding the sack which he had found by the railway track. 'Would you mind stepping inside?' asked the Inspector. 'A few too many prying eyes out here.'

Shaw saw the Inspector look disdainfully at the small knot of reporters who, realising a senior officer of some sort had arrived, had begun watching the two men on the platform. There was a flash of light and a loud 'pop' as one of the cameramen took a photograph of them from the station forecourt.

Shaw and Ludd went into the little station office, which was being used as a temporary operations room by the constables searching the track. The room smelled of coal dust and floor polish, and there was a constant round of 'excuse me's' and 'mind your backs' as policemen and station staff negotiated the narrow space.

Ludd spread the contents of the sack out on a battered wooden desk.

'Where exactly did you find this, sir?' he asked.

Fraser barked and Shaw quietened him while putting him under the desk.

'To be exact, Inspector,' replied Shaw, 'my dog found it. It was by the side of the railway tracks where the train stopped yesterday.'

'I see,' said Ludd, fingering his moustache. 'And what were you doing there, may I ask?'

'Going for a walk. It is a frequent route of ours.'

'Ours?'

'Fraser and myself.' Shaw pointed to the dog.

'Right. And is this the sack you said you saw the man threw into the undergrowth yesterday?'

'I believe it could be. Although I am not sure whether he threw it deliberately or dropped it accidentally. The fact that he paused for a moment in his flight suggests the latter.'

'It would seem that way,' said Ludd. 'We can't tell much from this lot,' he said, indicating the sack's contents of blonde wig, dress and high heeled shoes, and a diaphanous pink scarf. 'Dress has the label of an Ipswich department store in it. Probably sold thousands of them. Was this what you saw the woman on the platform wearing?'

'From the brief glimpse I had of the woman, I would say yes. Have you any idea what it all means?' asked Shaw.

'At this stage all I can say is that this goes some way to explaining what happened to the mystery blonde woman. This rather indicates there never was one.'

'I'm afraid I don't quite follow you, Inspector.'

'It sounds a bit of an odd question, I know, but are you sure the woman you saw on the platform *was* a woman?'

Shaw hesitated. 'If I understand you correctly, Inspector, you are suggesting that it could have been a man dressed as a woman.'

Ludd sighed. 'I think I must be getting like my sergeant, McPherson. He's prone to flights of fancy like this. It was a stupid idea.'

'No, Inspector,' replied Shaw. 'I think you may have a point. I did not see the face of the...person...on the platform. Though I did notice something else.'

'Yes?' enquired Ludd with renewed interest.

'I did notice,' continued Shaw, 'that the man running away from the train was of a small and slight build. With sufficient disguise, such a man could pass more easily as a woman than someone of, say, your height and build, for example'.

Ludd reddened. 'If you carry on like this, Mr Shaw, I may have to suggest you join my squad as a paid employee.'

Shaw smiled. 'There is one more thing, Inspector. Near to where Fraser found the sack, I noticed there were tracks in the grass and what looked like the tracks of a bicycle in the road. It may be of no relevance.'

'Or it may be extremely relevant. Thanks Mr Shaw, you've been very helpful, although I'm sure my lads will have noticed all that already.'

'Indeed,' said Shaw.

'But just in case they haven't perhaps we could drive up there in my car and have a look?'

'I will be happy to show you, Inspector, but perhaps it may be more beneficial to talk not to me at this juncture, but to the only other person, alive, that is, we know of who saw the mystery blonde'.

'That was the guard chap,' said Ludd. 'Good thinking. If I'm not mistaken I noticed him outside.'

Ludd looked through the sash window onto to the platform. There was a loud hiss of steam as the little shuttle train prepared to leave. He turned to a police constable next to him who was sipping tea from a tin mug.

'Get the guard off that train and in here quick smart.'

A few moments later, Watkins was standing in the little office with his railwayman's cap in his hands.

'I can't stop long sir,' he said, anxiously, 'we're off in five minutes.'

'Never mind about your timetable, Mr Watkins,' said Ludd impatiently. 'This won't take long. Now, you said yesterday the only other person you let into Cokeley's compartment was a beautiful blonde woman.'

'That's right sir, like a film star, she was.'

'What colour were her eyes?' said Ludd suddenly.

'Her...eyes sir? I, well, I don't know sir. She had on them glasses, like the girls in the magazines wear. Sun glasses, I think they calls them, sort of dark, like.'

'I see,' said Ludd. 'And did you notice what colour her lipstick was?'

Watkins paused. 'Well...tell the truth, I didn't see her face much at all. She had a sort of scarf on as covered most of it.'

'Like this, was it?' Ludd took out the scarf from the sack on the table.

Watkins' eyes brightened. 'That's the very same sir. Why, has that woman been found?'

Ludd pursed his lips. 'I have a feeling that we're not going to find her, Mr Watkins.'

He turned to the porter and ticket clerk who were bustling around a corner of the small office. 'Either of you two see a woman yesterday see a woman come through here wearing a scarf like this?'

The two men looked at each other then at Ludd. The clerk spoke first.

'I do recall a woman with that sort of scarf on, sir.'

The porter then piped up. 'So do I. Punched her ticket for the train yesterday. I remember it because she had it covering most of her face.'

'That's right,' said the ticket clerk, 'and she had on those glasses like the blind people wear. So's you couldn't see her eyes.'

Ludd sighed and turned to Shaw. 'So we're looking for a woman who has disappeared and whose face nobody actually saw. Mr Shaw, I'm beginning to think my theory might not be so fanciful after all'.

Chapter Eight

The black Morris Six squad car slid noiselessly to a stop at the end of the squalid little cobbled thoroughfare known as Railway Cuttings, Midchester. A police van blocked off the other end of the road, which was still quiet at this hour of the morning.

Detective Sergeant McPherson got out of the car and closed the door noiselessly; a slammed car door on a street like this could attract attention.

McPherson turned to the two constables emerging from the vehicle. 'Right lads. We'll go round the front and the other lot will go in through the alley at the back. Remember this West is wanted in connection with a murder so he may not be the type to come quietly. And remember, no rough stuff unless you have to. We don't want him up in front of a magistrate with two lovely black eyes, do we?'

'Don't worry sarge. We won't leave any marks on him,' said one of the burly constables with a chuckle.

'Hey,' admonished McPherson tersely. 'We're no' in Soviet Russia. We do this by the book. And it's Detective Sergeant, no' sarge.'

The constable looked crestfallen. 'Yes sar...I mean, yes,

Detective Sergeant.'

'Good man,' said McPherson. 'Right, let's go.'

He waved at the two officers at the other end of the short terraced street, who moved through the alleyway to the back of the house.

McPherson strode along the greasy pavement, littered with orange peel, cigarette ends and scraps of newspaper. He noticed a twitching of net curtains in the parlour windows of one or two houses, and hoped no warning would be given by the neighbours. He arrived at number 12, a small terraced house whose front door opened directly off the pavement. He then banged hard on the partly rotted door, which shook in its frame.

There was no answer, so he banged again, and this time called out.

'Reginald West, open up. This is the police'.

McPherson raised his fist to bang a final time when the door was flung open.

The imposing bulk of what he assumed was West's mother, or perhaps landlady, filled the door. Dressed in a dirty apron with her hair tied up in a turban and brandishing a mop, she demonstrated the impressive ability to shout loudly while retaining the stub of a lit cigarette in her mouth.

'Are you Reg's mother?' asked McPherson.

'Yus, sorry to say,' replied the woman. 'What you bleeding coppers want here? Reg 'as been clean as a whistle since he got out.'

'We're no' saying he hasn't,' said McPherson. 'We just want a wee word with him. Is he in?'

''Ave you got a warrant?' asked Mrs West, her narrow eyes peering suspiciously at McPherson through the blue haze of smoke rising from the cigarette in her mouth, which seemed magnetically attached to her lips.

'Look missus,' said McPherson impatiently. 'We've no' got a warrant. We just want a nice quiet word with your son. If we have to come back with a warrant we will, but it'll look the worse for him.'

'Gawd's sake,' breathed Mrs West, and turned towards the rickety narrow staircase behind her. 'Reg!' she bellowed upwards. 'Get up, that's the police 'ere to see you.'

She turned to the front door. 'Suppose you'd better come in,' she grumbled.

Seeing a neighbour looking out from the house opposite, she yelled out. 'And you can get inside an' all, nosey mare.' A face darted back behind grimy net curtains.

McPherson and the three constables with him trudged into the tiny hallway with its gloomy chocolate brown paint, peeling wallpaper and smell of cabbage; McPherson did not bother to remove his hat.

West appeared at the top of the staircase, wrestling his braces over his shoulders.

'Police want a word with you,' said Mrs West in an accusing tone. 'I don't want nothing to do with it.' She disappeared into the little back kitchen, leaving a trail of smoke behind her.

'Whatever it is you think I done, I never done it,' said West, guardedly.

'That would depend on what you think we think you've done, would it not, son?' replied McPherson with a grin.

'Alright then, what's it all about?' said West, as he trudged down the stairs and pushed his way past the men into the small front parlour.

He threw himself onto the shabby little sofa by the empty fireplace and lit a Woodbine cigarette from a crumpled packet pulled from his trouser pocket.

McPherson and the constables stood in front of him.

West glowered silently at them. 'We'll stand, thanks,' said the Scotsman drily.

'Suit yerself,' said West. 'And pardon me if mother don't make you a cuppa tea neither.'

'That's fine, son,' said McPherson.'We wouldn't want to outstay our welcome. My name's Detective Sergeant McPherson of Midchester CID, and I'd like to know where you were Wednesday afternoon, between twelve and two pm.'

'Why?'

'Just answer the question.'

'Can't remember, mate.'

'Try a bit harder then. And I'm no' your mate.'

'Alright, I was with a friend.'

'Has he got a name, this friend?'

'It's an 'er, not an 'im.'

'Oh right. Your old sweetheart, waiting for you faithfully after five years inside, was it? Or just some tart you picked up?'

West sneered. 'Why don't you go and…'

With lightning speed, McPherson cuffed West's face with the back of his hand.

West howled with indignation. 'You hit me!'

'That was just a wee slap, lad,' hissed McPherson. 'If I hit you you'll no' be able to talk afterwards. I did what I'd do to a puppy if it made a mess on the carpet. Now keep a civil tongue in your head and we'll get on just fine.'

'Alright, alright,' sniffed West. 'Yeah, I was with a tart. She works down at Maisie's.'

McPherson exchanged looks with the constables.

'The knocking shop? And we're supposed to take the word of someone who works in that den of iniquity?'

'Take it or leave it,' grumbled West, taking a deep drag on his cigarette. 'What you need to know where I was for, anyway? What am I supposed to have done?'

'Remember your old friend Charles Cokeley?' said McPherson.

'Who?' said West, with a puzzled expression on his face.

'You know who,' replied McPherson. 'The gent you did over, five years ago.'

'Oh, yeah, him,' said West. 'What's he want? I've done my time for that, they can't dredge all that up again.'

'You mean you haven't heard?' said McPherson.

West sighed and stubbed out his cigarette on the worn linoleum floor. 'Heard what?'

McPherson looked genuinely surprised. 'Do you no' listen to the wireless or read the papers?'

West folded his arms and glowered up at the policemen. 'We ain't got a wireless and I don't read the papers.'

'Don't or can't?' sneered McPherson. 'Well never mind, I'll tell you. Cokeley's dead. Someone stabbed him.'

'Lord,' exclaimed West sarcastically. 'Poor old soul.'

'Spare us the mock sympathy,' said McPherson. 'Thing is, he was robbed and killed in a railway compartment over Lower Addenham way. A very similar *modus operandi* to yours.'

'*Modus*…what?' asked West, his face twisted in annoyance.

'Did they no' teach you Latin at Borstal?' said McPherson. '*Modus operandi* means method of operation. And Cokeley was robbed using exactly the same method as you did last time, except this time he was killed.'

'Well I ain't got nothing to do with it,' said West, 'and you can't prove it. Just speak to Maisie or any of the girls down there and they'll vouch for me.'

Before he could reply, McPherson was interrupted by the sound of shouting and banging from the direction of the kitchen. Mrs West burst into the parlour rattling her mop and bucket, huffing and puffing indignantly.

'I ain't having it,' she exclaimed. 'They ain't got no right to go poking around my yard. You tell your men they ain't got no right. I got my mats airing out there.'

'You invited us in, Mrs West,' sighed McPherson. 'I told you we didn't have a search warrant so you could always have said no.'

'I don't mean you, I mean that lot in the back yard. One of them's knocked my best Axminster off the line and left ruddy great boot prints on it.'

'Alright, dear, we're leaving now anyway, I'll call the lads off,' said McPherson, turning to go.

Just then he was confronted by one of the constables assigned to watch the rear of the house. The man glanced into the parlour at West and then leaned towards McPherson's ear to speak in a low tone.

'I think you'd better come and have a look at the wash-house, Detective Sergeant.'

After he had showed Inspector Ludd the tracks he had found by the railway line, Shaw decided he ought to refrain from amateur detective work and instead concentrate on his parish duties.

After luncheon he strolled along the high street and stepped into Cokeley's antique shop, and again breathed in the aroma of musty upholstery and old furniture polish. Miss Ellis, the assistant, was at the counter, her thick horn-rimmed spectacles on the end of her nose, absorbed in reading some sort of ledger. Shaw cleared his throat. Miss Ellis jumped slightly, looked up and blinked through her thick spectacles.

'Yes?'

'Good afternoon. Miss Ellis, isn't it?'

'That's right. Can I help you?'

'I was rather hoping to see Mrs Cokeley.'

'What was it regarding?'

'A pastoral visit.'

Miss Ellis paused for a moment, then replied. 'I'll call her.'

As she turned to go into the little back parlour, she snatched up the large ledger and closed it quickly. Shaw noticed a long list of entries in red ink on the pages before it was snapped shut.

Miss Ellis disappeared and he heard her call up the stairs, followed by a muffled reply from a female voice. Miss Ellis returned into the shop and indicated to Shaw to walk around the side of the counter.

'Come this way please. Go up the stairs and turn right.'

'Thank you,' said Shaw. 'I know the way.'

After exchanging formalities, Shaw sat down in the little sitting room at the top of the stairs. Shaw noticed that this time, Mrs Cokeley hummed as she prepared tea in the little back kitchen, and she was no longer dabbing at her eyes with a handkerchief as she had done on his first visit. The dance band music emanating from the wireless seemed louder than before.

'I spoke with police this morning,' said Shaw, 'and they assured me that the necessary arrangements with your husband's body will be concluded within a few days.'

'Oh well that's a relief, I must say,' said Mrs Cokeley brightly. 'Some tea, vicar?' she asked, putting down the pot with its garish knitted cosy on the table.

Shaw took the cup offered to him and received the rather stewed looking brew.

'It is indeed a relief, Mrs Cokeley, but I must warn you,

that you will be required to identify your husband's body at the mortuary in Midchester. I will be happy to accompany you if you wish.'

Mrs Cokeley waved her hand airily. 'Oh, that's alright vicar. I'll manage. No, as I say, it'll be a blessed relief to get all this over and done with.'

'The murder investigation is likely to take some time, I fear,' said Shaw, sipping his tea.

'Oh I don't mean that,' said Mrs Cokeley. 'What's done is done. No sense worrying about investigations and such, I leave all that to the professionals. What I mean is, it will be a relief to get shot of this place.'

'This…place? I hope that your husband's death has not made you feel afraid to remain here?'

'Bless you vicar, me, afraid? I've got nothing to fear here. I'm sure it was that fellow West who killed Charles. You know, the one that robbed him last time. The paper said the police are looking for him. Once they find him that will be the end of that.'

'Perhaps,' murmured Shaw.

'No, what I meant was,' said Mrs Cokeley, who leaned forward and conspiratorially touched Shaw's knee, 'I'm getting shot of this place. This house. I've had a very good offer made for it. To sell up.'

'Indeed? And where will you go?'

'That's the lovely thing. I can stay right here in Lower Addenham. Or to be more precise, New Addenham.'

'New Addenham?'

'Yes, the new housing estate they're building down at the end of the village. It's them who's offered to buy this place. Well, Charles didn't want to sell, he kept upping the price even though I said he ought to take it. That nice Mr Symes was round and he was pleased as punch about it all. Said it was a relief for them to finally get this place.'

Shaw thought for a moment and then remembered that Symes was the man who, with some sort of business partner, had also been on the train the previous day.

'Yes, it's a funny thing really,' continued Mrs Cokeley. 'To think I'll be walking on top of where this old place used to be.'

'Walking on top?' exclaimed Shaw, with a puzzled expression.

'Yes, that's right. They're knocking this place down, the builders. That's why Mr Symes and Mr Davis are so pleased to be buying it. They said they stood to lose a lot of money if they couldn't, something to do with making a short cut to the station. Well, I don't mind telling you vicar, once they told me that, I thought why not get a good price? Of course I didn't ask as much as Charles wanted. But I did a deal with them.'

'A deal?'

'Yes, I asked for a discount on Anne Hathaway.'

Shaw finished his tea and put down his cup and saucer on the little occasional table next to him. He wondered what on earth the wife of William Shakespeare could possibly have to do with all this.

'Forgive me Mrs Cokeley. Anne Hathaway?'

'Yes, vicar. It's a house. One of the new ones they're building on the estate. You know the sort of thing, it's got up to look like an old place from the outside, but inside it's all mod cons.'

'Mod cons?'

'Modern conveniences. Oh, it's going to be lovely. Two receptions, downstairs cloak with H and C, and even a garage. Mind you, I haven't anything to put in it, but with the insurance policy I'll probably be able to afford something soon, although I'll have to take driving lessons. Goodness, just think! Me driving a motor car!' Mrs

Cokeley chuckled and slurped her tea.

Shaw stood up. 'I am pleased to hear that things are looking bright for you, Mrs Cokeley. I shall call again when I am able to provide an exact date for the funeral.'

Mrs Cokeley walked ahead of Shaw down the stairs, and he continued speaking.

'It is particularly interesting to hear about your husband's life insurance policy. On our previous meeting I was given to understand that it was somewhat... disappointing.'

'That's just it,' said Mrs Cokeley, as they entered the small back parlour behind the shop's counter. 'Mr Symes is ever so good with figures and that sort of thing. He offered to take a look at the policy and made some telephone calls and found out I'm due a lot more than I thought. And do you know, as another favour, he's going to have a look through my books.'

'Your books?' asked Shaw. 'Do you mean, antiquarian works?'

'No, bless you vicar, I mean the accounts for the shop. Frank, Mr Symes I mean, says he can't for the life of him understand why a place like this wasn't making more money. Thinks he might be able to get something back on taxes or the rates or something. Well, wonders will never cease. All in all I can't help thinking Charles' death was a blessing in disguise'.

Shaw could not think of anything to say to such a remark, and instead simply bid Mrs Cokeley good day.

As he passed through into the shop he noticed Miss Ellis frowning with a worried expression over the large ledger. He paused for a moment. She resembled...he could not think who it was, but somebody else that he had seen recently.

Miss Ellis looked up and saw that he was watching her.

'Forgive me for asking, Miss Ellis,' said Shaw, 'but may I enquire how you are bearing up?'

'Bearing up?' asked Miss Ellis with a quizzical expression. She quickly shut the ledger in front of her.

'Yes,' continued Shaw, 'after Mr Cokeley's death. It must have been quite a shock for you.'

'Oh, that,' replied the assistant quickly, pushing a wisp of dark hair back from her forehead. 'I'm quite well thank you'.

'A nasty business,' said Shaw, shaking his head. 'A respectable businessman killed for the sake of, what, a pound or two?'

Miss Ellis paused. 'Something like that I think.'

'Doubtless the police have spoken to you by now?'

'Yes,' said Miss Ellis tersely. 'I can't see what for. It was just an ordinary day and I gave Mr Cokeley a normal week's takings to the bank just as I always did.'

'The police have to be thorough, Miss Ellis, they will have asked similar questions of many people.'

'I suppose so,' replied the assistant. 'Well if you'll excuse me, I do have rather a lot of work to do.' She turned back to the ledger.

'Of course,' replied Shaw. 'Good day to you, Miss Ellis.' He put on his hat and left the shop.

'Well, well,' said McPherson, looking into the little brick wash-house in Reg West's squalid back yard. 'What have we here? He turned to the constable next to him. 'Bring him out.'

A few moments later the constable emerged from the kitchen door, holding West's arm firmly. The two men

91

crossed the weed-strewn patch of soil that passed for a garden. McPherson pointed through the doorway into the wash-house. 'These yours, are they?'

West's eyes widened as he peered into the gloom. 'What you talking about?'

'Well let's bring them out and give you a better look, shall we?' said McPherson. Taking care not to touch the handlebars, he lifted a man's bicycle out of the wash-house. 'Exhibit A. A man's bicycle with mud spatters on the frame and tyres.'

'So what?' said West nonchalantly.

'Is it yours?' said McPherson.

'Might be.'

'Mrs West,' shouted McPherson towards the house. 'Does your son own a bicycle?'

Mrs West appeared at the doorway and squinted at the bicycle. McPherson watched her and could tell she was in a dilemma as to what she should say. Finally she replied.

'Yeah, I think that's his. Why?'

'Never mind, thank you missus, you can go back inside now.'

Mrs West paused at the back step. 'What you been up to now, Reg?' she asked her son warily.

'I said thank you, you can go back inside,' said McPherson more firmly, and a constable ushered her back into the kitchen and closed the door.

'Ain't a crime to have a bike, is it?' asked West.

'A bike like that's not cheap,' said McPherson. 'Where did you get the money for it? You've only been out of stir a couple of weeks.'

'I had a bit saved up so I bought it.'

'Who from?'

'…I ain't saying any more till I speaks to a lawyer.'

McPherson laughed. 'And what are you going to pay a

lawyer with? The money you stole from Cokeley? Alright, look, son. To be honest I'm no' that interested in the bike. What I really want to know more about is this. Exhibit B.'

McPherson wrapped his handkerchief around his hand, lifted a brown leather bag out of the wash-house, and placed it on the ground in front of West.

'One Gladstone bag, leather.'

McPherson noticed West was nervously biting his lip.

'I never seen that before.'

'Let's have a look inside shall we?' said McPherson with a smile. He squatted down and tilted the open bag towards West. There was a sound of coins jingling. 'About seven pounds at least in there, I'd say. But what's really interesting is this writing here on the inside.'

McPherson pointed to an inscription in blue ink on the inside of the bag's canvas lining. 'Since I'm no' sure if you can actually read, I'll do it for you. It says "Charles Cokeley, 23 High Street, Lower Addenham, Suffolk"'.

McPherson stood up but immediately felt the ground give way under him as West shoved him in the chest and then broke free from the grip of the constable next to him. McPherson recovered his balance and made a grab for West, but the man had already got through the back gate into the alley beyond.

'Get them round here,' yelled McPherson over his shoulder. He careered into the alley and heard the shrill blast of a whistle from behind him, as one of the constables summoned help.

McPherson looked around and saw West sprinting up the narrow alleyway. He gave chase and was soon joined by the two constables who had circled round the side of the house.

McPherson skidded out of the alley into a small side road and paused to catch his breath as he realised West was trapped in a dead end; a brick wall about eight feet high blocked the end of the street. McPherson, his heart pounding, realised it was above the cutting for the main railway line into the city centre.

He called out. 'Come on son, you've had your fun now, let's get serious. We've got some talking to do.'

West called out but his voice was drowned out by the roar of a train passing through the cutting. McPherson's vision was obscured for a moment by clouds of steam bursting over the wall but when they cleared he realised that West had somehow climbed on to the brick structure and was walking gingerly along its top, with his arms outstretched to retain his balance.

McPherson could see what West was aiming for – an iron signal gantry a few feet away, projecting out from the adjacent brick wall on the side of the cutting. The fool is trying to get down onto the tracks, he thought.

Approaching the wall, McPherson realised that West had used the indentations in its crumbling face for foot and hand-holds.

'Here, give me a leg up,' he said to one of the four constables who had by now joined him.

'Are you sure about this, Sergeant?' asked one of them doubtfully.

'I said give me a leg up!' shouted McPherson and the policeman quickly complied. By pure instinct, McPherson followed in West's footsteps along the narrow crumbling edge of the wall and jumped the short distance onto the metal gantry. The rusty structure creaked and moved slightly as his weight hit it.

West was standing still on outside edge of the gantry, his knuckles white against the rusted black metal. McPherson, for the first time since climbing the wall, looked down and then recoiled with a dizzy feeling as he realised they were both perched about thirty feet above the railway line.

'I ain't goin' inside again,' yelled West defiantly.

'Don't be bloody stupid, son,' shouted McPherson, as another train roared past below. 'You'll never jump that. Do you want your ma to have to identify your body down there?'

McPherson looked to his right and realised that he could see over the wall to which the gantry was attached. On the other side the road was just a few feet below. West must have been so terrified that he had not even noticed the obvious escape route.

McPherson put out his arm. 'Come on son, I'll help you over.' West cautiously clambered back over the gantry railing and McPherson manhandled him over the wall where he dropped the short distance on to the road. Once there, he was immediately bundled into the police car that had just arrived.

Chapter Nine

Shaw walked along Lower Addenham's little high street for his late afternoon stroll, absorbed in thought. Inspector Ludd, it seemed, was confident that Cokeley's former assailant was the chief suspect, but the idea of him dressing in women's clothing seemed somewhat far-fetched to Shaw.

If that were not the case, though, how did one explain the discarded wig and woman's costume by the railway line? He also could not help thinking that Mrs Cokeley did not seem to be much of a grieving widow. He knew that they had been arguing of late and that Ludd had implied adultery may have occurred, but her attitude seemed not of one of loss, but rather of relief – almost levity.

Shaw stepped back suddenly from the kerb as a little Austin Seven whizzed past him, hooting its klaxon as it went. The modern world with its myriad sins is here even in this little corner of rural England, thought Shaw; the world of adultery, of robbery with violence, and fast motor cars that enabled strangers to come and go at will.

From the corner of his eye he thought he saw a figure standing in the doorway of Bland's, the butchers, but when he turned, there was nobody there.

Something was not right. He needed to think. A hymn

tune came into his head and he realised it was Sandys. Now, which one was that?, he pondered. Sometimes inspiration came to him in the words of hymns, but the words were usually preceded by the tune in his head.

Sandys...that was *Teach Me, My God and King*. Number two hundred and...forty or forty one in *Hymns Ancient and Modern*. Written by George Herbert. Fifteen-ninety something to sixteen something. Yes, that was it. He resolved to look it up when he got home.

As he reached the end of the row of shops on the high street, he had a distinct feeling of being followed. Although he did not believe in premonitions, sixth senses and the like, he did wonder whether the human mind had an instinct for impending danger which went beyond the normal senses. He had noticed it once or twice in France, before the Germans opened up an artillery barrage. One's ears seemed suddenly to hear more acutely and the hair on the back of one's neck stood up.

He turned again. There *was* someone following him. He caught a glimpse of a figure ducking into the hedgerow which lined the remainder of the high street on the way to the vicarage.

Shaw paused and stood still. As a clergyman, he was used to being approached by odd characters from time to time, his clerical collar seeming to act as a magnet to eccentrics, but that was less common here in the village where he was well known. He took out his pipe and began filling it.

He could see a pair of brown suede shoes protruding from under the hedge. He strolled closer and acted nonchalantly, placing his pipe between his teeth. Peering slightly round the hedge, he saw a man in a gaudy checked suit in the new double breasted style, with a wide brown trilby hat pulled down over his eyes.

'I say,' said Shaw to the man, with a tentative smile. 'I wonder if I could trouble you for a match. I appear to have run out.'

The man leaned slightly further back, and looked from side to side. He took out from his pocket a box of England's Glory matches, and passed it to Shaw.

'Here, keep the box,' said the man.

'Thank you, indeed,' said Shaw, striking a match and touching it to the tobacco in his pipe bowl. He looked the stranger up and down and realised that he recognised him.

'We've met before, I think?' said Shaw.

'Yes reverend,' whispered the man. 'On the station yesterday. After Cokeley got killed. I'm Joe Davis.'

'Ah yes, Mr Davis. A terrible business. I trust you are keeping well? Please feel free to speak to me if I can be of any assistance.'

'That's just it, reverend. I would like to speak to you about it.' Davis looked around again. 'But not here. Can we go somewhere?'

'Certainly,' replied Shaw. The George is just up the road.' He checked his watch. 'They will be opening shortly. Perhaps we might take a glass of beer?'

Davis licked his lips. 'Not the George. How about that little place just across from here. The, whatsit. The Bull.'

'As you wish,' said Shaw. 'Shall we walk together?'

'I'd rather meet you there in a few minutes,' said Davis, again in a low whisper. 'You go on, and I'll follow in a tick.'

Shaw smiled. 'Very well. Five minutes it is.'

A few minutes later, Shaw entered the little public house known as the Bull. Lower Addenham's main hostelry was the George, a former coaching inn which had been recently modernised in the mock-Tudor style, replete with fox hunting prints and electric lamp standards disguised as candles; it was a pleasant but somewhat soulless place, Shaw thought.

The Bull, on the other hand, was a far more traditional pub, low-ceilinged, perpetually dark and with high-backed wooden benches generally occupied by retired farm-hands who spent their days drinking and reminiscing about the old times.

'What can I get you, vicar?' said the heavily jowelled landlord, who was polishing glasses behind the bar.

'Good afternoon,' said Shaw. 'I believe the mild here is rather good.'

'Indeed it is sir. Brewed on the premises. Not many of us left doing that now. Mug or glass?'

Shaw chose the traditional option. 'A mug, if I might'.

'Certainly sir,' said the landlord, taking a pink china mug from under the bar and filling it with a dark mild ale from the pump.

'Nasty business about that antiques fellow yesterday,'

'Yes, quite,' replied Shaw.

'Mind, the police have made an arrest this morning. Just been on the wireless. I reckon it was that same feller done him over before, don't you? Well, it stands to reason, don't it?'

'Perhaps,' mused Shaw.

'That'll be tenpence ha'penny,' said the landlord, placing the mug on the bar.

Shaw handed over some coins and looked round for somewhere to sit. He saw an empty bench in the corner. As he walked over he saw an elderly man with a white beard without a moustache, who touched his forehead in the ancient feudal gesture of respect for a clergyman. Shaw nodded and smiled at him, then sat down at the bench and took a deep swallow of the nutty brown beer.

A few moments later, Davis walked in to the pub,

looking around furtively, with his hat still pulled down well over his eyes. Shaw smiled and wondered how the man thought he was being inconspicuous, particularly as he was wearing a loud checked suit and brightly coloured tie, making him about as inconspicuous as a music-hall comedian.

After ordering a double scotch from the barman, Davis sat down and raised the glass.

'Here's how, reverend.' He then swallowed most of the whisky.

Shaw raised his beer mug in return, and Davis leaned forward, again looking from side to side briefly before speaking.

'I need to talk to you about the murder'.

As late afternoon turned into evening, Ludd and McPherson were again seated at the table in the interview room at Midchester police station. Both men appeared tired as West was brought in by a constable, who pushed the prisoner down onto the chair facing them.

'Good evening, Mr West,' said Ludd. 'I hope you've had a chance to settle in to your new accommodation.'

'I hope you're feeling a bit more talkative as well now,' added McPherson, as he turned over a fresh page in his notepad.

West glared at the men silently.

'Let's go through a few things, shall we?' said Ludd. 'Where were you between twelve and two pm on Wednesday?'

'I already told him,' said West, nodding at McPherson.

'Well you can tell me now as well,' said Ludd.

'Down at Maisie's and then at home.'

'The tarts will vouch for you?'

'Don't see why not.'

'You're out of luck so far, son,' said McPherson. 'We sent someone round to speak to them yesterday but nobody answered. Maybe it was early closing day for tarts?'

West shrugged. 'Can't help it if they ain't answering, can I?'

Ludd leaned forward. 'Then there's the little matter of Charles Cokeley's bag. Containing,' he paused to consult his notebook, 'precisely seven pounds, fifteen shillings and ninepence. Quite a haul. That's about three week's wages for someone like you I'd say. Now, how did that come to be in your ma's wash-house?'

West shrugged again. 'I dunno. Most probably one of you lot planted it there.'

McPherson rose from his chair. 'You little…'

Ludd gently gripped McPherson's shoulder, and he sat back down. 'Thank you sergeant, let's remain calm, shall we? Now, West, I strongly suggest you don't mention something like that again, as I'll begin to think you aren't being very helpful. I don't think you realise how much hot water you're in. A convicted felon going back to rob the same man again and killing him this time. Juries tend to take a dim view of that sort of thing.'

'I never done it.'

Ludd leaned forward again and spoke slowly. 'Then start trying to convince me, lad.'

'Honest, I never seen that bag before,' said West with a scowl. 'I dunno how it got there.'

'What about the bike?' said McPherson. 'You told me that was yours.'

West paused, as if he was trying to think. 'So, what if I did? Ain't a crime to have a bike, is it?'

'No,' said McPherson, 'but here's the thing. Some tyre tracks were found in the mud near where Cokeley was killed. And guess what? They match the tyres on your bike.'

'And I reckon,' said Ludd, 'if we compare the samples of soil on the wheels of the bicycle it will match that on the road near the murder scene. I've got men working on that already.'

'That's what they call forensic evidence,' said McPherson. 'Now how do you explain that?'

West's eyes bulged and he swallowed rapidly. 'Alright, that ain't my bike. I lied about it.'

'Why did you do that, then?' asked McPherson.

'Cos I thought you were going to say I nicked it, didn't I?' whined West.

'Your mother said it was yours,' replied the Scotsman.

'Yeah, well, she was probably trying to protect me, weren't she? Honest, I never seen that bike before in me life.'

'How did it get in your yard then?' asked Ludd.

'Search me,' said West with a shrug.

'We'll be checking the handlebars for fingerprints to see if you touched it, mind,' said McPherson. 'So best you speak up now if you brought it in.'

Ludd noticed that West had gone as white as a sheet. The Inspector took out a packet of Gold Flake cigarettes and lit one for himself, then pushed the packet across the scarred table top to West.

'Have one. You look like you're gasping,' said Ludd.

West took a cigarette and lit it from Ludd's lighter, then took a long drag of smoke.

Ludd smiled. 'Alright, lad. Let's talk about something else. Do you ever dress up in women's clothing?'

West's eyes bulged again and he coughed up a lungful

of smoke. 'What?' he exclaimed.

'We're all men of the world here,' said McPherson. 'You can tell us.'

'What you on about?'asked West indignantly. 'I ain't one of *them*.'

'Prison can do funny things to a man, I've heard,' said Ludd.

'If I was one of them what would I be doing with the girls at Maisie's?' shouted West.

'Maybe getting some make-up tips off them?' said McPherson.

'Alright, lad, calm down, we believe you,' said Ludd. 'The reason I'm asking is this. The bike and the bag weren't the only things we found. We also found a woman's wig and clothing near the murder scene. We think whoever killed Cokeley, disguised himself as a woman.'

'Don't be bloody daft,' said West.

'Hey, don't you learn?' said McPherson angrily. 'Keep a civil tongue or I'll belt you again.'

'Alright, sergeant,' said Ludd. 'I think we could all do with a tea break. We'll have another chat in twenty minutes.'

'I'll have mine with two sugars,' said West, as the detectives got up.

'You're no' getting any tea until you start co-operating,' said McPherson. 'Now sit down and have a wee think about what you're going to tell us when we come back.'

A few minutes later the two detectives stood talking in the station canteen, sipping from their green institutional tea cups.

'What do you reckon, sir?' asked McPherson. 'Do we book him?'

'At the moment he's about the best hope we've got,' said

103

Ludd, ruminatively. 'Previous conviction for robbing the same man using the same M.O. Right height and build for the man seen running from the train. Found in possession of the victim's bag and money, and with a bicycle that is highly likely to have been used in the crime.'

'What more could you want than that, sir?' asked McPherson.

'Hmm, I don't know,' said Ludd. 'Just think what the papers will make out of it. Dressing up as a woman is a bit far fetched.'

McPherson smiled. 'You wouldn't say that if you'd had my first beat at Clydebank docks. Some of the sailors down there had some peculiar interests.'

'I'll take your word for it,' said Ludd with distaste. 'There's not much of that sort of thing in Midchester. But there's still the possibility of an alibi from the girls at Maisie's once we've managed to knock them up.'

'Knock them up, sir?' asked McPherson in a surprised tone.

Ludd grimaced. 'Don't be disgusting. I mean once we've managed to rouse them from their beauty sleep. I take it you've still got people trying, because if we don't get an answer soon I want that door down. They should be put out of business anyway.'

'Aye sir, we will. But who's going to take the word of a few tarts, compared to all the other evidence? He could have paid them to perjure themselves anyway, out of the money he stole. He might have taken more than seven quid, for all we know.'

Ludd paused and looked into his teacup. He was acutely aware that the next few moments might be the beginning of a process that could mean life or death for West.

He mentally reviewed the other suspects; a mild-mannered parson, a clapped-out war veteran with one leg, a train crew all with impeccable records; two slightly suspect property dealers from London, but they didn't strike him as the robbing and murdering type.

Of course, he thought, it could have been just some random lunatic by the railway line, who seized his chance when the train was stopped at a signal, or someone totally unconnected that they didn't know about, but what was the likelihood of that happening? No, he thought. All the signs pointed to West.

'Well sir?' asked McPherson.

Ludd drained the last of his tea and plonked his cup and saucer down decisively on the table. 'Get back down there and charge him'.

In the Bull, Davis had started on his second double whisky of the day. 'I don't quite know how to put this, reverend,' he said, nervously fingering his glass, 'but I think I might know who killed Cokeley.'

Shaw was about to mention the wireless report of an arrest being made, but something stopped him. He attempted to conceal his interest by puffing in an dispassionate way on his pipe.

'That is surely a matter for you to discuss with the police, Mr Davis.'

Davis flushed. 'Ah, well, you see, me and the law, well, we've had our differences in the past. What I mean to say is, I'd rather not talk to a copper unless I have to. The police and I haven't tended to see eye to eye on certain financial matters.'

'We are talking of a murder, Mr Davis. If the killer is not found, he might very well go on to kill again. I think it is your duty to tell the police what you know.'

Davis looked exasperated. 'It's not just that I don't want to talk to the coppers, it's just that, well, I don't want to have to finger a mate.'

'Finger a mate?' asked Shaw in a puzzled tone.

'Let me put it another way, reverend,' said Davis. 'Thing is, I'm not of one of your lot so I'm not quite sure where I stand with you. I'm what you might call Church of Turkey.'

Shaw smiled at the old army expression used by those with no religious connections. 'I consider,' replied Shaw, 'those of your denomination to be just as much members of my flock as anyone else'.

Davis took a swig of his whisky and looked furtively around the empty tap-room. 'That's very nice of you and all, reverend, but what I really mean is, am I right in thinking that if I tell you something in the box, you can't tell anyone who told you. Sort of an anonymous tip-off, like?'

'Forgive me Mr Davis.' said Shaw, putting down his pipe and then swallowing a long draught of ale. 'I'm not with you. What box are you referring to? A telephone kiosk?'

'Telephone? No, you know, the what do you call it. The…confession box.'

'Mr Davis, I am a minister of the Church of England. Aside from a small minority who lean heavily towards Rome, we have not used confessionals since the Reformation. The confession of sin is generally considered a private matter between you and your maker'.

Davis appeared disappointed. 'So you mean there's no get-out clause for squealing on a mate?'

'There is obviously something troubling you, Mr Davis. The sacrament of confession is not recognised in my denomination, but nevertheless, the seal of confession is still practised. To put it in layman's terms, if you truly wish to unburden yourself of something, that information will remain entirely confidential.'

'So you won't go telling the law, then?' asked Davis, an expression of relief crossing his face.

'As I said, anything that you wish to remain a matter between ourselves, will remain so. May I suggest that we continue this discussion in a more private place, such as the vicarage, or perhaps the church vestry?'

Davis looked worried again. 'I'd rather not reverend. I shouldn't be here anyway, as I'm meant to have just popped out to the dentist. I can't risk being seen anywhere out with you.'

'Very well. Then please tell me what is on your mind.'

Davis took out a cigarette and tapped it vigorously on a silver case before lighting it. 'Well,' he said, while exhaling a large cloud of smoke upwards, 'it all started when I spoke to old Goggins in the George today when I was having my lunchtime pint. You know him I think?'

'Yes. I have not had a chance to speak with him since he was released from police custody. Is he quite well?'

'You know these old soldiers, Reverend. Tough as old boots. He's alright. But he told me something very interesting as we were talking about the murder.'

'Go on.'

'He said the police were asking about some blonde piece who got into the compartment with Cokeley.'

'Yes,' replied Shaw after a pause. He wondered just how much information he ought to reveal, but then decided he was perhaps over-thinking matters. 'I also saw her.'

'You didn't catch a look at her face, did you?' asked Davis.

'No. It seems she has not been identified, nor was any

trace of her seen once the train had arrived at Great Netley.'

'It's a pity you didn't see her face,' said Davis. 'I'll be straight with you, reverend,' said the salesman, looking around the bar furtively. He took a large sip of whisky and smacked his lips. 'I don't quite know how to put this but I think my business partner and our secretary might be tied up in all this.'

'Once again I must remind you Mr Davis that this is a matter for the police.'

'And once again reverend, with all due respect, I'm not going to the law. At least until I get a bit more evidence. I just want to know if you think I'm on the right track.'

'Very well, Mr Davis. Please tell me your theory.'

'Alright. Well, I've been having my doubts about Frank – that's Mr Symes – for a while. Me and him, well we're both bachelors, and lodge in rooms at the George, but lately he's been keeping odd hours and he's not been down for our usual game of cards in the evenings.'

Shaw smiled. 'Perhaps he has a sweetheart?'

'That's just what I'm worried about. See, Frank's been thick as thieves with the secretary, Ruth Frobisher, recently. And the other day she said something about having to carry out "extra-curricular duties" or something.'

'I have no desire to pry into your colleagues' private lives,' said Shaw. 'What intrigues me however, is why should this have anything to do with the death of Mr Cokeley?'

'I'm coming to that. Alright, so maybe he's just having…er…relations, with Miss Frobisher. He wouldn't be the first or last man to do that I don't doubt. But old Goggins told me the police were looking for a blonde woman. Reckon she got into Cokeley's compartment and distracted him, or did him over herself, or something.'

'I fail to see the connection.'

'Ruth Frobisher's blonde, and a tasty bit of goods as well, if you'll pardon the expression, reverend.'

'Attractive young women with blonde hair are not unknown in England, Mr Davis.'

'Alright, but what about this. Now this is something you've really got to keep under your hat. We've been trying to get hold of Cokeley's property for ages, to build a shorter access road to the new housing estate, but he wouldn't sell.'

Shaw took a large sip of beer. 'Let me guess. Cokeley's death now puts you both in an advantageous position.'

'That's right. And I want to make it clear Symes stands to make a lot more than me. I'm just an employee, really. If the estate doesn't get built it's not much skin off my nose, but if this project doesn't work out for Symes he'll end up bankrupt.'

Davis seemed anxious to unburden himself, thought Shaw. Perhaps the man was aware of how Cokeley's death might incriminate him as well as Symes. He allowed him to continue.

'Cokeley's wife's always been more keen to sell up than him, and now it should be a piece of cake. It was Symes that had the idea of going into Great Netley on the same train and cornering him in a pub to and have a final go at persuading him to sell. But here's the clincher, Symes said something about "solving the problem of Mr Cokeley for good."'

'I see,' said Shaw, somewhat doubtfully. 'Mr Davis,' he continued, 'do you have any affinity with the detective stories of Miss Christie, or Miss Sayers?'

'Detective stories? Don't think so. *Racing Post*'s about all I read.'

'I admit to a certain indulgence in them myself from

time to time,' explained Shaw. 'And one thing I have learned is that suspicion of an individual involves three things: means, motive and opportunity.'

'I'll take your word for it.'

'If we assume the acquisition of Cokeley's house as the motive, and the train journey to Great Netley as the opportunity, that leaves only the means in question.'

'What do you mean by means, exactly?' asked Davis, lighting another cigarette.

'To put it another way, how do you think he was killed?'

'I've thought about that as well,' said Davis quickly. 'Fact is, well, Tuesday night we had a bit of a late session in the George, so by Wednesday afternoon I was feeling a bit sleepy and nodded off for a few minutes in the train. When I come to, I saw Symes sliding shut the window, he said there had been some shouting outside and that we'd stopped.

'Well, I didn't think any more about it until poor old Cokeley got found dead at the station. But it was this blonde bit of stuff that made me suspicious. What if Symes got Ruth to distract Cokeley while he bumped him off?'

'But how,' said Shaw, draining his glass, 'did Symes manage to, as you say, bump him off?'

'What if he climbed out of the compartment while the train was stopped, ran along the track, got in, stabbed Cokeley then came back? He could have been coming in just as I woke up, and that was why he was at the door.'

Shaw paused, again wondering how much information he should reveal. He decided against mentioning the man who had been seen running on the track as well as the wireless announcement of the arrest of a suspect.

'So what do you think, reverend?'

Shaw knocked out his pipe into the ashtray. 'I think neither of us can do much at this time. If you are not willing to divulge to the police what you have told me, there is little that I can do. Except perhaps to meditate on it in prayer.'

'I don't want anyone thinking I'm mixed up in all this, including Him upstairs.' Davis looked up briefly then fixed his eyes on Shaw. 'I'm not much of a praying man, but I'll be grateful if you could put in a word for me while you're doing it.'

Shaw got up to go. 'I shall, Mr Davis. Rest assured, I shall meditate considerably on what you have told me.'

As Shaw walked home in the gathering dusk, he suddenly remembered the words of the hymn that had come into his mind earlier.

A man that looks on glass
On it may stay his eye
Or, if he pleaseth, through it pass
And then the heaven espy.

Would Inspector Ludd, he wondered, 'stay his eye' on the most obvious suspect, or would he 'through it pass' and then the 'heaven', or in this case, ultimate truth, 'espy'? Shaw was beginning to think there was certainly a lot more to this case than he first thought.

Chapter Ten

'I am the resurrection and the life saith the Lord: he that believeth in me, though he were dead, yet shall he live: and whosoever liveth and believeth in me shall never die.'

Shaw intoned the time-worn sentences from St John's Gospel as he led the funeral procession from the lych-gate into the church, and as he did so, he was conscious of the weight of centuries pressing upon him. These words from the Prayer Book, he thought, must have been uttered countless times before in this place in a similar manner, and no doubt would be spoken again over countless funerals to come.

Cokeley's funeral was a brief affair. Mrs Cokeley was dressed in mourning black, but seemed composed and almost bored during the service. Her husband, it seemed from the sparse turn-out, had had few friends or relations. A cousin had made the journey from Midchester, and Shaw also noted, with some surprise, that Goggins was sitting at the back of the church, with his arms folded and his face expressionless.

The rest of the congregation consisted mainly of the elderly spinsters of the village who enjoyed a 'good send-off' and who would always attend a funeral, if only because of the likelihood of some free refreshments afterwards.

They had no such luck at this particular send-off. Mrs Cokeley had told Shaw that she didn't like funeral receptions, describing them as 'nasty gloomy affairs with everybody arguing about what they should be inheriting'.

After the brief service in the church, Shaw spoke the final collect over the grave in the corner of the little churchyard:

'We meekly beseech thee, O Father, to raise us from the death of sin unto the life of righteousness; that, when we shall depart this life, we may rest in him, as our hope is this our brother doth; and that, at the general Resurrection in the last day, we may be found acceptable in thy sight...'

Would Cokeley, Shaw wondered, a cheat and a philanderer, and probably an adulterer as well, be found acceptable in His sight? He prayed earnestly that he might be, but that justice might also be done.

The prayers finished, the little knot of mourners began to drift away and the sexton began shovelling earth onto the coffin. Shaw noticed that the two bored looking reporters with cameras, who had been watching from beyond the churchyard wall, had disappeared. He accepted Mrs Cokeley's cursory handshake.

'Thank you so much vicar, that was a lovely service, nice and short.'

'Thank you Mrs Cokeley,' replied Shaw. 'And once again, if I may be of any assistance to you, please do not hesitate to ask.'

'You've been wonderful, vicar. But don't you worry about me. I know it sounds awful but I still can't help thinking Charles' death was a blessing in disguise. For me anyway. It's a chance for a new start.'

Shaw chose his next words carefully. 'Indeed, there are blessings in every circumstance, if we would but look for them.'

'"Every cloud has a silver lining"', that's what Frank, that's Mr Symes, says,' replied Mrs Cokeley cheerfully.

'Oh that reminds me,' she added, 'I must be getting back to the shop as we'll be going through the accounts in the week and finalising the sale. I'd invite you back for a cup of tea vicar, only I'm walking cousin Ernest to the station and then it's *Variety Band Box* on the wireless.'

Before Shaw had a chance to reply, Mrs Cokeley strutted off briskly, taking the arm of Cokeley's elderly cousin and almost frog-marching him in the direction of the station. Shaw smiled as he heard Mrs Cokeley admonishing him.

'I've already told you, Ernest. Charles didn't say anything about that Wedgewood vase you keep mentioning so if you want it you'll just have to pay full price like anyone else'.

'She's not exactly the grieving widow, is she?'

Shaw looked up to see Goggins standing next to him.

'Good afternoon, Mr Goggins. I didn't notice you by the grave just now,' said Shaw.

'I kept my distance,' said Goggins. 'Didn't want to get too involved as he was no friend of mine. But I don't want anyone thinking I didn't turn up because I had some sort of grudge against him.'

'And why would anyone think that, Mr Goggins?'

Shaw heard a familiar voice from behind him, and looked round to see Inspector Ludd standing by the graveside, with his hands behind his back.

Goggins bridled. 'I thought I was in the clear with you lot,' he said.

'You are, for the moment,' replied Ludd. He nodded at Shaw.

'Mr Shaw.'

'Good afternoon, Inspector,' replied Shaw.

'I was in the area and I thought I'd drop by to let you have the good news. We've charged Reg West with Cokeley's murder. Although you've probably heard that by now anyway.'

'It was in the newspaper,' said Shaw. 'I understand West was the man who previously robbed Mr Cokeley. The incident occurred shortly before I became the incumbent here, so I know very little about it.'

'Well I just hope they've got the right man this time,' grumbled Goggins. He said a curt 'good afternoon' to Shaw and limped off towards the road, ignoring Ludd entirely.

Ludd watched the man go and then turned to Shaw. 'Oh, and thank you again for finding that sack,' he said. 'I've got men checking the department stores to see if anyone remembers selling the wig and clothes and so on. It could be useful if one of them can put the finger on West.'

'You're convinced West is the killer?' asked Shaw.

'Seems like it to me. Now we've got to build up a case and that means getting as much evidence as possible.'

'I see.'

'Yes,' said the Inspector, drawing himself up and holding the lapels of his raincoat in the manner of a barrister. 'I think we're going to get enough to nail him. That's mainly why I'm here. I've got men checking the line again for any more clues they might have missed first time round. Some more bicycle tracks, perhaps.'

'Ah yes,' said Shaw. 'I understood from the newspaper report that some evidence had been found regarding those.'

'Yes, that's another thing I have to give you credit for, sir,' said Ludd. 'You spotted those bicycle tracks in the mud by the railway line. Well, they're an exact match for the tyres of a bicycle we found in West's back yard.'

Shaw nodded. 'There was also mention that Mr Cokeley's money bag was found with it. It would seem to be somewhat damning evidence.'

'It puts him in the frame alright,' said Ludd proudly.

'Forgive me Inspector, but one thing puzzles me,' said Shaw. 'As I understand it, your theory is that West may have disguised himself in women's clothing to gain access to Cokeley's compartment.'

'That's right. It sounds a bit queer, I'll grant you, but stranger things have been heard of.'

'Indeed. After killing and robbing Mr Cokeley, presumably West then changed back into his ordinary clothes, exited the train and then made his escape by bicycle.'

'Well done, Mr Shaw,' said Ludd with a smile, still clutching his raincoat lapels. 'I see you have an analytical mind, like mine.'

'Perhaps,' said Shaw. 'But, if your theory is correct, what puzzles me is how West knew that the train would stop at the exact spot where he had left his bicycle for his getaway.'

'I'm one step ahead of you on that one, Mr Shaw,' said Ludd. 'It seems obvious to me how he did it.'

'You have the advantage of me, Inspector.'

'Yes, it's my belief he studied the timetables of the trains and knew that the local had to stop at that signal to let the London express pass through further up the line.'

'It seems cleverly planned. But from what I recall of the previous robbery of Mr Cokeley, it was done on the spur of the moment.'

'It may well have been the first time. But he's a clever one, this West. He's putting up a good job of convincing us he had nothing to do with it. But remember, he's had five years inside to plot this one.'

A chill spring wind with the promise of rain swept through the churchyard, sweeping Shaw's greying hair away from his forehead. He shivered.

'Since there is no funeral reception, Inspector, perhaps you might like a glass of sherry at the vicarage? One does not like to be nosey, but it is fascinating to discuss the details of such an intriguing case with you.'

Ludd frowned. 'Thanks all the same Mr Shaw, but I'd better not; I'm on duty. And I'd better be getting back to my lads on the railway line.'

'Of course.'

'So thanks once again, and perhaps you'll drop a line into your sermon this Sunday to assure your parishioners they can sleep soundly in their beds. I'll stake my pension on West being the killer.'

Shaw smiled. 'I will bear that in mind Inspector. Good day to you.'

Once Ludd had gone, Shaw stepped into the relative warmth of the little parish church and walked into the vestry, pausing only to bow from the neck in front of the altar. Once inside the little room he took off his cassock and surplice and changed into his usual three piece suit of dark grey tweed.

Had he gone too far in inviting the Inspector for a glass of sherry, he wondered? It was tempting to play the amateur detective, of the type one read about in yellow-back novels, but he reminded himself that this was Saturday and he ought to prepare himself for Sunday, the busiest day of his working week.

As he walked from the church over to the vicarage, however, he could not help thinking again of Herbert's hymn. 'A man that looks on glass, on it may stay his eye...'

117

Was Ludd looking on glass when he said he would stake his pension on West being the killer? Shaw shook his head to rid himself of such speculations. He had a sermon to complete.

'Did the funeral go well, Lucian, dear?' asked Mrs Shaw, as the clergyman hung his hat in its usual place on the hall-stand. When Hettie had first started as their maid, she had asked if she should perform that function for him. It seemed ridiculous to Shaw to pass a hat to a maid only for her to hang it on a peg two feet away, so he had instructed her to leave that ceremony for visitors only.

'As well as might be expected,' sighed Shaw, as he kissed his wife on the cheek and bent down to pat Fraser, who jumped up in excitement at seeing his master return home. 'A sad business,' he said, shaking his head.

'I know dear,' said Mrs Shaw. 'Anyway perhaps this will cheer you up.' She picked up a parcel wrapped in newspaper from next to the hall stand. 'It's a rather jolly picture I spotted in Cokeley's shop.'

She unwrapped the parcel and displayed the picture to Shaw. He smiled as he realised it was a watercolour painting of a Norfolk scene, the same picture he had thought of buying her for her birthday.

'You see, it's already cheered you up,' said Mrs Shaw brightly. 'I thought it would be at least a small help to Mrs Cokeley to buy something from her. And it will cover that damp patch by the door there very well'.

She held up the picture to the wall, concealing a patch where the Regency striped wallpaper was discoloured.

'It's very pretty, my dear,' said Shaw.

'And it wasn't at all expensive. Only fifteen shillings.'

'Strange,' said Shaw. 'The ticket says five shillings. You're not trying to cheat me out of the housekeeping money, are you?' he asked with a smile.

'Don't be silly dear. No, that was a mistake, according to the girl.'

'Miss Ellis?'

'Is that her name? Yes I think so. Well anyway, she said it was priced wrongly and ought to have been fifteen shillings. I did wonder about refusing as that sort of thing does annoy me rather.'

'What sort of thing?' asked Shaw.

'Shop assistants who get muddled with prices. It's not the first time she, I mean, Miss Ellis, has done that. Do you remember that little silver bell I bought in there, so that we could ring for Hettie?'

'I believe so. I recall at the time being rather amused that such a thing was necessary in a house of this size. We could simply shout for her, or clap our hands twice, as the Arabs do.'

'Oh you are silly, Lucian. Yes, it rather annoyed me that she said the price of that was wrong as well. It was definitely a few shillings more. So it was such a disappointment when the same thing happened with the painting, and I was going to leave it, but then I thought of poor Mrs Cokeley and decided an extra ten shillings might help her. And it's such a pretty scene, don't you think?'

Shaw did not reply. His attention had been caught by newspaper that had been used to wrap the painting, and which was now lying on the hall-stand.

'I said isn't it a pretty scene, Lucian?'

'Er, yes, quite, dear, quite. I say, may I have this newspaper?'

'Of course, but what on earth for? It's weeks old.'

Shaw picked up the torn paper. 'To, ah, light the fire in the study.'

'A good idea,' replied Mrs Shaw. 'I'll tell Hettie to lay it. It's turned rather chilly so don't stint yourself, we've plenty of coal, they delivered far too much last time anyway.'

'Very well, I ought to get on with my sermon.'

'Of course dear,' replied Mrs Shaw. I'll leave you in peace.'

Shaw closed the door of his study behind him and smoothed out the newspaper on his desk. It was the local Midchester paper from a few weeks previously. He scanned the headlines until he found the one that had caught his eye in the hall. Yes, there it was: 'Addenham train robber released'. Beneath the headline was a blurred photograph of a young man with a sullen expression, which Shaw assumed was what was known as a 'police mug shot'. He read on.

> Reginald West, 26, of 12, Railway Cuttings, Midchester, was released from prison yesterday after completing a five year term for robbing and assaulting businessman Charles Cokeley in a railway carriage. The attack shocked the village of Lower Addenham where Mr Cokeley is a respected antiques trader. Mr Cokeley was unavailable for comment but his assistant, Miss Sybil Ellis, 29, said West's release was 'an unpleasant reminder of something we'd all rather put behind us.'

Shaw sat back and lit his pipe, puffing thoughtfully as he stared through the window into the garden. There was something, he thought, not quite right about all this, despite Inspector Ludd's belief that the case was all but closed.

He did not believe in mystical insights, but he did

believe that the Almighty worked His purpose out through His creatures. He had thought before that he ought not to play at being a detective, but now he was not so sure.

He was interrupted from his reverie by a knock on the door; it was Hettie, come to lay the fire. He resolved to put the matter out of his mind until Monday, his day off, and took out his fountain pen to make the final adjustments to his sermon.

Chapter Eleven

'Blooming Monday again,' sighed Symes as he hung his raincoat on the peg near the door of the estate office. 'Had a good weekend, Joe?'

Davis, who had come in to the office a little earlier than usual, looked up from his copy of *The Sporting Life*.

'Eh? Oh, not bad thanks Symsie, not bad. Didn't see you at the George.'

'The George?' replied Symes airily. 'Oh, no I wasn't around much. Had a few things to catch up on.'

'Busy, eh?' said Davis, lighting his first cigarette of the day. 'How about a cup of tea? Where's Ruth? It's gone nine now.'

Symes sat down at his desk. 'She overslept, I assume.'

Davis tutted. 'We've got to sort that girl out. She swans around as if she owns the place.'

'Give over will you?' said Symes, shuffling through some papers on his desk. 'I need her on side at the moment.'

'Oh, why's that?' enquired Davis, with a suspicious expression.

'Old dame Cokeley likes her, that's why. They get on

like a house on fire, talking rot about the wireless and women's things and what-not.'

'Women's things?' asked Davis with slight alarm in his voice.

'Yes, you know,' replied Symes. 'Make-up, clothes, that sort of thing. And right now we need all the help we can get with that Mrs Cokeley.'

'Why's that?'

'I think she's taking a leaf out of her husband's book. She's umming and ah-ing about what we're offering her for the house. I can't afford to pay her any more.'

'I thought she was happy with the offer.'

'She was but now she seems to think she's not as well off as she was. Lord knows why. Anyway, I told her I'd be round with Ruth today to go through her books. Hopefully we can convince her to accept our price.'

'Hopefully,' mused Davis. 'Or we're stumped.'

'We will be,' replied Symes. 'We got lucky with Cokeley but we're not likely to be as lucky a second time.' Symes straightened his tie and ran a hand through his hair. 'Ah, here she is,' he exclaimed.

Davis looked up to see Miss Frobisher enter, filling the little office with the aroma of her cheap perfume.

'You're ten minutes late, dear,' said Davis with annoyance.

'Oh, am I?' said Miss Frobisher lightly. 'I got, erm, held up.'

'If you say so Ruth,' said Symes. 'Now, let's have a nice cup of tea before we tackle Mrs Cokeley.'

Davis folded his paper and cast a suspicious glance over the pair as they both smiled at each other in what seemed to him to be a conspiratorial manner.

Shaw always kept Monday as his day off. He enjoyed the sense of calm after the feeling of being on show all day on Sunday, from the early Holy Communion service through to Evensong, having to deal with the myriad 'quick words' that his parishioners wanted to have with him.

He sometimes envied the unchurched, who spent their Sundays lazing in bed or reading the newspapers or drinking in public houses or working on allotments, but reflected that such a life must ultimately be unfulfilling. It was the calm sense of having nowhere to go and nothing to do that he really liked, and he was content to be able to achieve that on at least one day a week.

This particular Monday, however, Shaw *did* have somewhere to go. His unease over the murder case had been building all through Sunday, and he had felt his mind starting to wander during the Evensong collects. A prayer recited perfunctorily, he always thought, was no prayer at all, and so he decided he would try to put his mind to rest on one or two matters.

Mrs Shaw was out on her usual Monday excursion for morning coffee with the village ladies at the Tudor Tea Rooms. She called it 'taking Fraser for a walk' but the little dog rarely got much exercise, having to sit quietly under the table where he eyed the more pampered lapdogs of the parish with suspicion.

Shaw stepped into the small back kitchen of the vicarage. 'Just going out for a while, Hettie,' he said to the maid, who was busying herself with the breakfast washing up. 'I'll be back for luncheon'.

'Right you are sir,' said Hettie, taking her hands out of

the sink and drying them on the roller towel.

'Oh and sir,' she added, 'Madam asked me to hang that picture so I've put it up in the hall next to the door like she asked. Good job you've a picture rail there as I'm no good with a hammer.'

Shaw stepped into the hallway to look at the painting.

'Thank you Hettie. Well done.'

Hettie then walked up to the picture. 'Oh I'm ever so sorry sir,' said Hettie. 'I've left that little tag that says five bob on it.'

Shaw looked at the small ticket on a short length of string which hung from beneath the picture.

'That's quite alright, Hettie. As a matter of fact, that's reminded me of something. Good day to you.'

He smiled and opened the door, taking his hat from the hall-stand as he went out.

As he strolled down the high street, Shaw noticed a man and woman walking towards Cokeley's shop. He realised it was the estate agent, who worked with Davis. Shaw remembered his name after a moment: Symes. The woman was a young, attractive blonde and Shaw realised this must be the Miss Frobisher that Davis had mentioned. Before he came close enough for them to see him, they disappeared into the gloom of the antique shop.

Shaw walked on until he came to the railway station. There did not seem to be any reporters there now; presumably they had moved on to new scandals elsewhere now that a suspect had been charged with the murder.

Shaw entered the vestibule of the station and was pleased to see that Ambler, the black-clad and grimy train driver whom he had spoken to a few days earlier, was on the platform, oiling the wheels of the little engine which sat waiting, hissing and creaking.

There did not appear to be anyone else around so he

stepped on to the platform and bade good morning to the driver.

Ambler squinted at Shaw and then smiled as he recognised the clergyman. 'Ah, morning vicar,' he said. 'Off to Great Netley again are you? It'll be a few minutes yet before we leave.'

'Good morning Mr Ambler,' said Shaw. 'I enjoyed my little tour of your engine so much the other day. I must confess to being something of a railway enthusiast.'

'A lot of parsons seem interested in trains, they say,' said the driver. 'I reckon it's because a parson and a train driver are both concerned with keeping everybody on the straight and narrow, and not letting anyone fall by the wayside, so to speak,' He chuckled at his own joke as he continued oiling the train wheels.

Shaw smiled politely. He was not generally amused by clerical humour.

'Indeed, very apt. What interests me is not just trains, but railways in general. I believe we previously discussed signals.'

Ambler paused. 'I recall that we did. I can't say I've ever had much interest in those apart from what I has to, but it takes all sorts to make a world, they say. Well, this branch has only the one signal at the mainline junction, to tell me to give way if there's a mainline train going through. As I mentioned last time, that one's controlled by the signal box at Great Netley.'

'I see,' replied Shaw. 'Most interesting.'

'Funny you should mention that again,' replied Ambler. 'Those policemen were asking me about that the other day, after the murder. They asked me why I'd stopped the train that time and I said, well, I had the stop signal, didn't I? Nothing more to it than that. Perhaps he thought we'd got bandits on the line, like in the American films.'

'I suppose you always have to stop there?' asked Shaw.

Ambler wiped his hands on an oily rag. 'That's the odd thing. I don't recall that particular service has to stop at that signal for a London express. One of the morning trains does, but not that afternoon one. But it could be that there was a hold up on the London line, or a special going through.'

'A special?'

'Yes, sometimes they lay on an extra train that's not on the timetable, to take people to a football match or summat. Get a few games on Wednesday afternoons, don't you? So that could have been it. I don't work the main line and I don't follow the football, so I wouldn't know. But the police fellers seemed satisfied with that explanation anyhow.'

'I see,' said Shaw, turning to go. 'You've been very helpful, Mr Ambler. I shall let you get on with your work.'

'Tell you what, vicar,' said Ambler. 'If you really wants to know more about signals, hop on and I'll take you up to Great Netley and introduce you to the lads at the box. They might even let you have a look around.'

'That really is most kind of you,' said Shaw. He turned to go. 'I shall purchase a ticket.'

Ambler winked. 'Don't worry about that, vicar. You get up here in the cab with me.'

Shaw smiled. 'Thank you. I shall be most interested to see how it all works.'

Chapter Twelve

A few minutes later Shaw was fulfilling a childhood dream of riding on the footplate of a railway engine, crammed into the little cab with Ambler and Webb, the fireman. The noise, heat and smoke were far greater than he could have imagined, and he dreaded the scolding he would get from Mrs Shaw when she saw the soot on his clerical collar. The high point for Shaw was being allowed to pull the whistle to give a merry toot as the train passed over the little pedestrian level crossing just outside Lower Addenham.

As they approached the lone signal on the line, he noted the short distance between the railway track and the road. Anyone fleeing from the train to a waiting bicycle, he realised, would have had only a short distance to run before making good his escape.

Ambler turned to Shaw and spoke, raising his voice almost to a shout to make himself heard.

'This was where they think the murder happened, wasn't it? I saw that young feller run off the train across the fields there,'– he pointed to his right – 'but I never thought he'd done a murder.'

Shaw replied, raising his voice also. 'Did you say he was on the right hand side, Mr Ambler? The man I saw ran from the left side of the train, down to the road.'

'Don't know anything about that,' said Ambler. 'The chap I saw was on the other side of the train, running for his life across the fields back to Addenham.'

Shaw's mind was suddenly in a whirl. He decided now was not the best time to distract the driver with questions, so he bided his time until the train arrived at Great Netley station.

After Ambler had eased the train to a halt, turning various wheels and pulling several levers, he turned to Shaw.

'I hope you enjoyed that, vicar.'

'It was splendid,' replied Shaw. 'And thank you, also, Mr Webb,' he said to the fireman. 'If you'll kindly point me in the direction of the signal box, I shall be on my way.'

'I'll walk you over there, vicar,' said Ambler, wiping his hands on an oily rag which seemed to have the effect of making them appear dirtier rather than cleaner. 'I don't have a great deal to do until the run back, and George here will get her ready.'

The two men walked along the platform in the opposite direction to the handful of passengers who had emerged from the little train.

'Forgive me, Mr Ambler,' said Shaw, 'but I feel I ought to be sure about what you said just now about the man we saw running from the train. As both of us may be called to testify in court over what we saw on the day of the murder, it would do well to be in agreement over which side he ran from'.

'Sing from the same hymn sheet, as it were, eh vicar?' said Ambler with a grin.

'Quite,' replied Shaw. 'A defending barrister could make good use of confusion over such matters.'

Ambler frowned as the two men stopped walking and

stood together on the narrow wooden platform.

'You mean I might have to be up in court?'

'It is highly likely that we both will be called upon to testify. Could you recognise again the man you saw?'

Ambler thought for a moment. 'Not rightly, no. I only saw him from behind, like.'

'I see. Now, the man I saw ran from the train on the left side, past the signal and onto the road. Yet you say the man you saw ran from the right side of the train, across the fields back to Lower Addenham.'

Ambler's eyes narrowed and Shaw noticed dark lines of soot embedded in the creases around them.

'Well all I can say is this,' said the driver. 'The fellow I saw was definitely running off from the right.'

'And you told this to the Inspector?'

Ambler paused. 'You mean the fellow with the moustache asking the questions here the other day? No, I never spoke to him. After he'd been talking to you and the others he shot off and left the talking to an ordinary bobby who took some notes. Come to think of it, all *he* asked was if I'd seen anybody running away from the train and I said yes. I don't think he asked me which way he was running. Just told me they might have to speak to me again and that was that. I thought they'd have wanted to know a bit more but they didn't seem to. For all they know I could have done the chap in myself.'

Shaw smiled at the notion. 'Presumably with Mr Webb the fireman as your partner in crime? I find it rather unlikely.'

'Next you'll be saying that mystery blonde woman that disappeared off the train was my gangster's moll!'

Ambler laughed but then turned it into a cough, presumably as he remembered he was talking to a clergyman.

'But speaking seriously,' said Shaw, 'it is certainly rather intriguing. Either one of us is wrong about where he saw the man, or…' His voice trailed off.

'Or,' replied Ambler, raising his eyebrows, 'there were two men.'

Miss Ellis, plainly dressed as usual in a shabby and unflattering tweed suit, was sitting in her favourite place at the counter of Cokeley's shop, poring over two large ledgers. She occasionally made marks in one of them with a pencil, while referring to the other. Dance music from Mrs Cokeley's wireless drifted down from the upstairs flat.

She looked up as the front door opened and a man and woman walked in. She recognised the man as Mr Symes, the rather odious fellow who was something to do with the estate agency down the road. He was almost as lecherous as Cokeley, she thought to herself.

She had also seen the brassy blonde woman before – some sort of secretary, she assumed – and had noted with distaste her peroxided hair and tight-fitting frocks. Miss Ellis wondered whether she had to put up with lecherous behaviour from her employer as well. Perhaps she even enjoyed it? She had heard some women did.

'Yes?' said Miss Ellis to the couple, in a cold tone of voice.

'Good morning my dear, and how are you this fine day?' responded Symes warmly. His type always said things like that, thought Miss Ellis. She ignored the attempt at flirtation.

'May I help you?' she asked.

'You could help me by putting a smile on that pretty

131

face,' said Symes, taking his hat off and turning it in his hands in front of him.

Miss Ellis felt herself blush and hated herself for it. She noticed the blonde secretary eyeing her with what looked like pity.

'Never mind him, dear,' said the secretary. 'He's a brute like most men are, aren't you?'

Symes chuckled and leaned closer to Miss Ellis, who shied away from him in distaste.

'And that's just what you ladies love, isn't it, Miss…?'

'Ellis. What do you want?'

'These, for a start.' Symes leaned forward and scooped up the ledgers on the table.

'Put those back,' said Miss Ellis angrily. 'Those are private company accounts,' She felt herself blush again.

'Alright love, keep your hair on,' said Symes, replacing the books on the counter. 'That's why we're here. Old Ma…I mean, Mrs Cokeley, has asked us to go through a few things to do with the shop accounts. I'm sure she'll be down for those ledgers later. Is she in?'

'Wait one moment. I will see if she is available,' said Miss Ellis primly. She got up and turned to walk to the staircase but was confronted by Mrs Cokeley in the doorway.

'Oh, good morning Mr Symes, and Miss Frobisher,' trilled Mrs Cokeley, who was puffing on a cigarette in a holder.

'You're looking particularly lovely today, Mrs C,' said Symes unctuously.

'Oh you do flatter me, Mr Symes,' replied Mrs Cokeley with a girlish giggle. 'Won't you please come through?'

Miss Ellis glared at the pair as they passed by her and followed Mrs Cokeley up the stairs.

'Here's the signal box, vicar,' said Ambler, as he and Shaw reached the end of the platform at Great Netley. Shaw felt a childish thrill as he was allowed to proceed through a little wooden gate, with a metal sign attached which warned of a fine of five pounds for anyone caught trespassing on the railway.

Ambler led the way up a flight of metal steps on the outside of the little white-painted wooden building, which had large windows facing out on to the tracks. The driver pushed open the door and called out cheerily. 'Morning Bert, morning Graham.'

Two men were standing at a row of large, waist-high metal levers beneath the windows of the little building. The older man smiled in recognition at Ambler, but the younger man, a portly, red faced youth, was absorbed in the effort of pulling one of the levers forward.

'I've bought an interested party along, Bert,' said Ambler. 'This here's Reverend Shaw from down the line at Addenham. Reverend Shaw, Bert Fox.'

'Good morning, sir,' said Fox, who, thought Shaw, with his stocky build and grey beard was distinctly un-fox-like in his appearance. 'Oh and this here's Graham, Graham Moffatt, my assistant.' He pointed to the younger man, who nodded silently at Shaw.

'Nothing wrong is there, Perce?' said Fox. 'Only we don't often get parsons in here. Nobody's died, I hope?' he added with a chuckle.

'Now that's not in very good taste, is it Bert?, chided Ambler. 'Considering what happened last week.'

'Ah of course, how could I forget?' said Fox. 'No

disrespect intended. They've caught the fellow who did it, I heard.'

'The police have charged a man, that much is true,' said Shaw. 'But fear not, I am not here on clerical matters. It has always been a desire of mine to see how a signal box operates, and Mr Ambler was kind enough to invite me to look around.'

'Well I've been on the signals all me working life,' said Fox, 'so it don't seem like anything special to me, but I'm happy to show around a friend of Percy's. It's quite straightforward really.'

Shaw wondered what could possibly be straightforward about the little room with its array of levers and detailed maps and timetables on the opposite wall.

'These here levers control all the signals along the line here between us and Lower Addenham, and a mile or so each way to Ipswich and Midchester.'

Fox pointed to a linear map on the wall showing the locations of signals. 'I keeps an eye on the timetable and Graham operates the signals. It's a young man's job really, as pulling them things all day fair tires you out.'

An electric bell tinkled from somewhere in the room. Fox consulted his pocket watch and said 'London line clear now, Graham.' The young man heaved on a lever and there was a metallic clunking noise from below the floorboards of the room.

'How on earth does it work?' asked Shaw.

'It's all done by hydraulics,' explained Fox. 'There's a hydraulic system under here that forces a cable along the side of the line, and that operates the signals and the points up to a mile away.'

'Fascinating,' said Shaw. 'It never really occurred to me how it all works. If asked, I would probably have thought each signal had its own operator stationed by it, rather like policemen on traffic duty.'

Fox chuckled. 'That was how they did it in the old days, when the trains was slow and there was only a few lines, but you'd need hundreds of men for that now,' he said. 'And they'd be stood out in the cold and wet all day, poor beggars. '

Suddenly an electric bell mounted on the wall above the signal levers rang three times. Fox ran his finger down a printed timetable on the wall.

'Wake up Graham,' called out Fox to his assistant, who was dozing over the levers. 'Heavy goods from Netley West coming through.'

'Righto,' said Graham, and pulled one of the signal levers down.

Fox then turned to what looked like a telegraph operator's switch under the bell, and tapped it three times.

'Now see what happened there, vicar,' said Fox. 'That's the goods train coming up from London. It's just passed through the next station to us, Netley West, so the box there lets us know with a signal through that there electric bell, and so we changes the signal and points here to let it through. Then I taps ahead up the line to the next box. And so on, all the way up the line to Norwich.'

'But, to the best of my knowledge there is no signal box at Lower Addenham,' said Shaw. 'How therefore are you notified of an oncoming train from there?'

'Ah, I see you're an observant man, vicar,' said Fox. 'Well, Lower Addenham's on a branch line. It only goes from here to there and back again. There's only the one little train on it that just goes back and forth, see. So all that happens when the train leaves Lower Addenham is the station master sends me the signal via his telegraph bell that the train's left. Right, Percc?'

'That's right,' replied Ambler. 'pushing buttons while

sitting on his backside is about all that lazy beggar's good for.'

Fox and Ambler both laughed.

'A most impressive system,' said Shaw with a smile. 'But would it be possible to operate a signal manually, from outside this box?'

'Well technically yes, vicar,' replied Fox. 'The cable can be operated manually at the signal, but you'd only do that for maintenance or some such. There's a fail-safe weight on 'em, so that if anything goes wrong they drop down horizontal, which means stop.'

'So in theory a signal could be operated without your knowledge?' asked Shaw.

Fox paused. 'In theory sir, yes.'

'Is that not rather dangerous?' said Shaw. 'What if trouble makers, nuisance-mongers and the like were to alter the signals? It could cause havoc. '

'I recall that was done in Ireland during that nasty business a few years back,' mused Fox. 'But it's unlikely here. For a start you'd have to know how to do it, and there's a special key that only us signalmen have, to do it with. So any Fenians or what-not wanting to cause trouble would have to get one of those keys.'

'I think I see what you're driving at, vicar,' said Ambler, who up until now had been quietly smoking a short, dirty pipe while he stared out of the signal box window. 'You're thinking somebody deliberately stopped that train last Wednesday so's they could rob and kill that poor fellow.'

'I must admit the question had entered my mind,' said Shaw cautiously.

'I highly doubt it though,' said Ambler. 'More likely it was a special or an excursion passing through the main line so Bert here gave the order for the train to stop. Ain't that right, Bert?'

Fox chuckled. 'I don't know every blooming train off by heart, I'm not God Almighty, am I? Pardon me, vicar.'

Shaw smiled. 'Now that you mention it, it may be of interest to the police if you were able to find out whether the train last week received a stop signal from here.'

'Police?' said Fox with surprise. 'What they want to know about my signals for?'

'Indulge me, please, Mr Fox,' said Shaw. 'Did you give a stop signal to the, now what was it, yes, the 12.55 from Lower Addenham to Great Netley, on Wednesday last?'

Fox sucked air through his teeth as he ran his finger down one of the timetables on the wall. '12.55. 12.55, now let me see…there's no scheduled main line service then. The 12.55 should have come straight through onto the main line to here, without needing a stop signal.'

'I knew it,' said Ambler. 'We don't normally stop at that signal. Could have been a special though.'

'A special?' asked Shaw.

'Yes,' said Fox. 'But I usually gets a separate notification of specials, which I pins up on the board here. I don't recall getting that. Only thing I can think of was it was a delayed train coming through. Probably up from Ipswich. They've been having work on the line there. I don't recall though.' Fox called across the box to his colleague. 'Can you remember anything, Graham?'

Graham mumbled something indistinctly.

'Speak up, lad,' said Fox.

'I said that were the day I was ill.'

'Ah, that's right, I remember now,' said Fox. You *was* off sick, or so you said. Probably hung over, more like, weren't you?' he said with a good natured laugh.

'I don't drink, Mr Fox,' said Graham, blushing furiously.

'Anyway,' continued Fox, 'I had to run the box on my own for that afternoon shift. I thought about sending for young Jack, that's Jack Ellis, my other assistant signalman, but Wednesdays and Mondays is his days off and I had no way of getting in touch, so I says to myself, "Foxy, you're on your own today."'

'Did you say his name was Ellis?' asked Shaw.

'Yes, that's right,' said Fox. 'Lives over your way. Perhaps you know him? But then again I think he's chapel'.

'Ellis...' pondered Shaw. 'Does he happen to have a sister?'

'Think so,' replied Fox. 'He's mentioned a sister. Here, didn't she work for that fellow as was murdered last week?'

'I believe that may be her,' replied Shaw. After a pause, he continued.

'Did Mr Ellis mention anything of the murder?'

Fox shook his head. 'What, Jacko? No, he's a quiet one, him. Keeps himself to himself.'

'Probably on his best behaviour,' interjected Ambler. 'Got into a spot of bother a year or so back, didn't he?'

Fox bridled at this comment. 'It was nothing more than high spirits, a bit of drunk and disorderly, the police let him off with a warning and so did the station master. Water under the bridge.'

'My lips are sealed, Bert,' said Ambler in an admonished tone.

'Anyway, as I was saying, vicar,' continued Fox, 'if I *did* stop the train you're talking about, it was most likely because of a late running train up from Ipswich. But I must admit I can't remember rightly, with all the running about I was doing. If it's really important I suppose I could find out for you.'

'Please don't trouble yourself, Mr Fox,' said Shaw. 'It was really only a matter of private interest. Now I ought to let you two gentlemen get on with your work.'

'Right you are then vicar,' said Fox. 'It's been nice talking to you. Any friend of Percy is a friend of mine.'

Ambler opened the door of the box for Shaw, who walked out into the cool air, full of the smells of soot and smoke from passing trains.

Fox gave a cheery wave. 'Any time you need to know about signals, vicar, you come and see us. Good day to you!'

Shaw travelled back to Lower Addenham on the next train. Throughout the brief journey he reflected on what Fox had told him in the signal box. He felt a queer mental sensation of loose ends gathering together, a sensation he had sometimes felt when preparing a sermon on a difficult topic, such as the nature of the Trinity. He decided that he ought to try to speak to Inspector Ludd before proceeding.

As the train slowed to a halt at Lower Addenham, Shaw noticed a small crowd of people outside the station, and two police cars parked in the forecourt. A number of police constables were milling around, and one was manning the station barrier.

As Shaw alighted from the train, he noticed the police constable speaking with a heavy-set man in a belted raincoat with a bowler hat pushed back on his head. He realised it was Inspector Ludd.

The Inspector spotted Shaw approaching and broke away from the constable.

Shaw resolved that he would take the opportunity of this chance meeting to mention his theories on the case.

'Good morning, Inspector. A lot of activity, I see. Have further developments in the case occurred?'

'You can certainly say that, Mr Shaw,' said Ludd, with a frown. 'Mrs Cokeley's dead. Looks like she's been murdered.'

Chapter Thirteen

Shaw felt as if he had received a blow to the stomach. A physical pain almost; a sensation he remembered from the trenches when the news of yet another young soldier's death was relayed to him.

'*Another* murder?', asked Shaw incredulously.

'Certainly looks like it,' said Ludd. 'She was found in the shop a couple of hours ago with a knife through her heart.'

'Good Lord, this is terrible,' said Shaw.

'Tell me about it,' said Ludd. 'And just when we thought we'd got her husband's killer bang to rights. Well, we know it can't be him that did it, as he's currently sitting in a cell in Midchester. But we'll find this one too. I've got men on the barrier here questioning anyone taking the train out, and I've put roadblocks on both sides of the village.'

'I see,' replied Shaw. 'Then I shall not detain you any longer, Inspector.' He touched the brim of his hat and made to leave the station.

'Just a minute, if you don't mind, Mr Shaw,' said Ludd. 'now that you're here, you could be of assistance to us.'

'Of course, Inspector. I am at your disposal.'

'Being a man of the cloth, you'll be good at, what do

they call it, pastoral care.'

'I don't quite follow.'

'Consoling people in times of distress, and all that.'

'I see. Yes, that is indeed one of the duties of a parish priest.'

'Yes, well, that girl who works in Cokeley's shop, Miss Ellis, is beside herself. Can't stop her crying and we can't get anything out of her. It was her that discovered the body. I've tried to get a WPC over from Midchester but there's none available apparently.'

'WPC?' asked Shaw.

'Woman police constable,' replied Ludd. 'Shoulder to cry on – everyone's favourite auntie, you know the sort of thing. Can't really have any of my men trying to do that.'

'Quite. And in the absence of such an...auntie, you believe I may be of use? Would it not be better if I fetched my wife, perhaps?'

'I'd rather it was you, sir. I wouldn't want Mrs Shaw to have to, well, witness the sights in the shop, so to speak.'

'Very well. I will be glad to be of assistance'.

'Is Miss Ellis one of your lot, sir?' asked Ludd.'

'My lot?' enquired Shaw in a puzzled tone.

'I mean, is she a church-goer?' said Ludd.

'I do not recall seeing her at church. I believe her people may be Methodists. But be that as it may, I find in times of trouble a clergyman of any denomination can be of consolation.'

The two men made their way out of the station towards Cokeley's shop. A little group of what Shaw assumed were newsmen were standing on the pavement, held back by two police constables. Across the road a small crowd of villagers were gathered, murmuring and pointing. Once again he felt sick to his stomach that the peace of the little community could have been disturbed in such a way.

They entered the shop, which seemed to Shaw to have a more sinister and gloomy air than he had noticed before. Perhaps it was the overcast weather, or perhaps the recent visitation of violent death.

Miss Ellis was seated on an overstuffed armchair – price £1/10/-, Shaw noticed on the little label attached to it. She was dabbing her eyes with a handkerchief and staring at the ground, as a young police constable stood awkwardly by her.

Beyond, through the doorway into the small parlour at the back of the shop, Shaw could see something on the ground covered with a sheet. He realised that must be the late Mrs Cokeley. Two men were talking in low tones by the corpse, one whom he recognised as the other detective – McPherson. The other man appeared to be some sort of doctor, he thought, judging by the stethoscope around his neck.

'Miss Ellis,' said Ludd quietly, 'I've brought the vicar to see you. Thought a familiar face might help.'

The shop assistant looked up with red rimmed eyes. At first she did not seem to recognise Shaw but then whispered a reply. 'Oh, it's you, vicar.'

Shaw pulled up a chair (George III, price £1/19/6, according to the tag) and sat close to Miss Ellis.

'I realise this must have been a terrible shock for you, Miss Ellis,' said Shaw. 'But please try to answer the questions of the police. The killer could still be at large and it is vital that he be apprehended as quickly as possible.'

Miss Ellis sniffed and blew her nose. 'Yes, of course,' she said in a resigned tone. 'I'm sorry, it was all such a shock. I just couldn't face such a flurry of questions.'

Ludd, who was standing close by, shifted his weight from one leg to another, awkwardly. Shaw guessed he was not comfortable dealing with distressed persons.

'Of course. Perhaps you could simply tell us in your own words what happened,' said Shaw.

'I...I'll try,' said Miss Ellis. 'I went out for my lunch hour. I usually sit and eat my sandwiches in the back room here. But Mrs Cokeley had told me to go out as she was having a private meeting upstairs. I got the impression she wanted me out of the way.'

'A private meeting with whom?' Shaw spoke gently, and noticed that Ludd was quietly taking notes behind Miss Ellis.

'Those two from the estate agents down the road,' said Miss Ellis with a sniff. 'I saw them come in, but I can't remember their names. A man and a woman...wait, it was Mr Symes and Miss...Frobisher. Yes, that's it.'

'Symes and...Frobisher.' Ludd repeated the names under his breath as he made a note in his pocket-book. He leaned forward closer to the armchair.

'What time was this, please, miss?'

'I...I'm not sure. About twelve, I think.'

'And what did they do?' asked Ludd.

'They met Mrs Cokeley and went upstairs. A few moments later Mrs Cokeley came downstairs again and told me to go out for lunch.'

'And did you?' asked Ludd.

'I did but I thought it was a little strange,' said Miss Ellis. 'I normally just shut the shop up for the lunch hour and eat my sandwiches in the back. But Mrs Cokeley was quite insistent that I should go out. She said she had to get back to her business meeting upstairs.'

'I see,' said Ludd. 'And where did you go?'

'I sat on the little bench in Back Lane,' said Miss Ellis. 'I thought the weather might brighten up again but it didn't. I sat for an hour and came back and then I found...I found...' She buried her face in her handkerchief.

'You found what, Miss Ellis?' asked Ludd.

'I found Mrs Cokeley…dead…in the back room. And then I telephoned for the police.' She then broke down in a fit of sobbing.

'I think perhaps I ought to take Miss Ellis home,' said Shaw.

Ludd coughed. 'Yes, alright. Thank you, Miss Ellis, you've been very helpful. We will need to speak to you later to get a formal statement, of course.'

Shaw helped Miss Ellis on with her mackintosh as Ludd opened the shop door and stepped outside. Just then a young man sprang forward through the police cordon around the shop. A constable tried to take his arm but he shook it off, and shouted 'I told you, I want to see my sister.'

Ludd shut the door behind him and blocked the doorway. 'I'm sorry sir…' protested the constable, but Ludd cut him off.

'It's alright thank you, I'll handle this,' said Ludd, turning to the young man. 'Now, what's all this about?'

'I said I've come to see my sister. Somebody just told me there's been a murder in her shop. I need to see if she's alright.' He tried to push past Ludd into the shop doorway.

'Alright, alright son, calm down,' said Ludd, barring the way. 'First things first. What's your name?'

'Jack Ellis. My sister Sybil works in there.'

'Just a moment,' said Ludd. He opened the door and called inside. 'Miss Ellis, do you know this man?'

Miss Ellis and Shaw stepped forward. The woman ran into her brother's arms. 'Oh Jack,' she blurted. 'Thank God you're here.'

'And thank God you're alright,' said Ellis.

'Perhaps you'd be good enough to take your sister

home,' said Ludd. 'She's had a bit of a shock.'

'Of course,' replied Ellis. 'Come on Sybil, I'll walk you back.'

'Oh and there's just one more thing before you go, miss,' said Ludd. 'Can anyone vouch for you sitting on the bench in Back Lane between 12 and 1?'

There was a pause. Miss Ellis then looked at her brother. 'Of course. I was with you, Jack, wasn't I?'

Ellis looked directly at Ludd and Shaw. 'That's right,' he said quickly. 'She was with me the whole time.'

'Once again you've been very helpful miss,' said Ludd. 'Now please go home and get some rest.'

'But what about the shop?' said Miss Ellis. 'Do I come back in to work tomorrow?'

Ludd frowned. 'I don't think so. You take a few days off at home. We'll keep an eye on this place until we sort things out.'

Shaw stepped forward to speak. 'And please do not hesitate to call at the vicarage if I can be of any assistance.'

'Thank you but it really won't be necessary,' said Miss Ellis.

'As your parish priest, I feel I am duty bound,' said Shaw, firmly. 'I, or my curate, will endeavour to visit you in the next few days.'

'I really don't think that's…I just want to go home,' said Miss Ellis, her voice breaking.

'Come along sis,' said Ellis, gently as he took her arm. 'Let's get you home.'

Shaw stood in the doorway of the shop and watched Miss Ellis and her brother walk away up the high street.

'Poor girl,' said Ludd. 'It's enough of a shock finding a dead body, but then she's just realised she's probably lost her livelihood as well. Anyway, thanks for that, Mr Shaw, helps to have a friendly face with a witness, sometimes, especially of the female variety. Us coppers are intimidating at the best of times.'

'That is quite alright, Inspector,' said Shaw. 'But I wonder if I might have a moment of your time to discuss a matter of some importance connected with the case.'

'Oh yes? Step inside the shop, would you?'

The two men went back inside and Ludd closed the door behind them.

'Just give me a minute will you?' said the Inspector. 'I need to convene with McPherson and clear up a few things then you'll have my full attention.'

'Very well, Inspector, I shall wait for you here,' said Shaw, who sat down again on the Georgian chair. He was tempted to smoke his pipe, but, just as when he had been waiting for the Inspector after Cokeley's murder, he felt perhaps it would be inappropriate, and contented himself instead with looking at an early Victorian prayer book which he found on a display case.

He found his attention wandering as he overheard Ludd and the Scottish detective, McPherson, talking in the back room.

'Well, one thing's for sure,' said Ludd in a disappointed tone, 'it wasn't West, because right now he'll be sleeping off his lunch of bread and water in the station cells.'

'Aye but who was it then, sir?' asked McPherson. 'No signs of forced entry or theft or anything like that as far as I can see. Doesn't seem to have been an ordinary robbery.'

'You're not in Glasgow anymore, lad,' said Ludd. 'An ordinary robbery in a town like this is a kiddy taking some sweeties while the shopkeeper's back is turned.'

'Aye maybe, sir,' said McPherson. 'But what if West is still connected with it somehow? What if he's working with someone else?'

'Alright,' said Ludd. 'We'll grill him about that later. But right now I want you to find this pair from the estate agents. They were in here about twelve apparently. Symes, and a woman called Frobisher. I assume it's that wooden hut place down the lane just before the Ipswich Road. I want to know what they were doing here and when they left. Take a couple of men with you, and bring them in to the station if you have to.'

'Right sir,' replied the Scottish detective briskly, and he made his way out through the front door, nodding to Shaw as he passed. Shaw watched as the man strode over to a police car parked opposite the shop, and began speaking to the driver.

Shaw then heard Ludd speaking to the other man in the back room. Looking around briefly, he recognised him as the police doctor who had examined Cokeley previously.

'Knife through the heart, Inspector,' said the doctor blandly. 'Just like that last one. Been dead a couple of hours, I'd say.'

'And not a bayonet this time,' said Ludd, peering at the handle of the weapon protruding from Mrs Cokeley's chest. 'Looks like a paper knife or some such. I want this fingerprinted as soon as possible,' he added.

'Not until I've done the post-mortem please, Inspector,' said the doctor. 'I don't want your men poking and prodding around before I've had a chance to.'

Ludd sighed. 'Very well doctor. But let me know as soon as you're done.'

There was a moment of silence as the two men looked at the corpse.

'Dead a couple of hours, you say?' mused Ludd. 'It's gone two o'clock now,' said Ludd. 'We got here at one forty-five. Miss Ellis said she found the body just after one. So Mrs Cokeley would have been killed just after twelve?'

'I'd say that's about right,' said the doctor. 'Of course, I

147

can't be completely sure but the physical indications strongly suggest that.'

'I see, thank you, doctor,' said Ludd. 'You can take her away now. Let's do this discreetly, out the back way. I'll go and fetch a couple of my lads to help you.'

'Of course, Inspector, thank you,' replied the doctor.

Ludd emerged from the back room. 'My apologies, Mr Shaw,' he said. 'As you can see we've got our hands full at the moment. Now, what was it you wanted to speak to me about?'

Shaw stood up. 'I realise you must be very busy, Inspector. And you are probably aware of this already. But I couldn't help overhearing your sergeant mention the possibility that the killer could be an accomplice of West. It was of interest because I have been wondering that also.'

'Look, Mr Shaw,' said Ludd with a slight tone of impatience. 'I appreciate your help with Miss Ellis. But right now I don't really need any theories from the public. No disrespect, but you should hear some of the stuff people come up with during murder cases. We even get people confessing to them who have got nothing to do with it.'

A few days ago Shaw would have felt admonished by such a rebuke, but with all that he had heard and seen, he felt duty bound to continue.

'Of course, Inspector,' he said. 'I would not dream of simply airing fanciful theories; your time is far too valuable, as is mine. But I happened to speak to Mr Ambler, who told me something rather interesting.'

'Ambler? I know that name. Wasn't he the one driving the engine when Cokeley got killed?'

'That is correct.'

'What were you talking to him for?' asked Ludd suspiciously.

Shaw smiled. 'As a vicar, I speak to all sorts and conditions of men, Inspector, just as you do, albeit in perhaps a more spiritual capacity.'

'Of course,' said Ludd. 'I realise that's part of your job, or I wouldn't have asked you in to help with Miss Ellis. Go on.'

'Well,' said Shaw. 'As you will see in my statement to you, and also I think in that of the guard, the man we saw running from the train was on its left hand side, as one faces the engine.'

Ludd ruffled through the pages of his notebook until he found the relevant page. 'Yes, that's right,' he said. 'What of it?'

'Mr Ambler claims that the man he saw was running from the right hand side of the train, as one faces the engine.'

Ludd turned the pages of his notebook rapidly. 'Alright,' he said. 'I think one of my constables took a brief statement from them. I was engaged on other matters. I'll have to compare notes when I get back to the station. Thanks anyway, Mr Shaw.'

'You are most welcome, Inspector,' said Shaw. 'May we conclude from this, that there are indeed two men involved?'

'It's possible,' sighed Ludd. 'But it's also possible that whatsisname, Ambler, got it mixed up. People get their stories confused sometimes and swear blind they saw something when they didn't, and vice versa.'

'As the modern Biblical scholars frequently remind us,' said Shaw with a wry smile.

'Er, yes, quite,' said Ludd, with the wary look on his face that Shaw recognised as that of awkwardness around spiritual matters.

'Well it's interesting to hear your theories, but I must be

getting along now Mr Shaw,' said Ludd, so if you'll excuse me...'

'Of course Inspector. I might add though that I have no desire to waste your time with my theories. My concern is for my parishioners. If a killer is on the loose, he may kill again, and as their clergyman I will be called upon to reassure them.'

'Of course, Mr Shaw,' said Ludd. 'If it's of any help, I think that it's highly likely West *is* working with an accomplice, and I'm also pretty confident we'll find out who he is pretty soon. I don't think this is some lunatic killing at random. That might be scant reassurance for your parishioners but at the moment it's the best I can offer.'

'Thank you Inspector,' said Shaw. 'That is indeed reassuring.'

The two men left the shop under the watchful eye of the police constable on the door, and hurried to their respective destinations, away from the gaze of the growing huddle of newspapermen on the road opposite.

Chapter Fourteen

If the murder of Mr Cokeley had created a sensation in the village, the murder of Mrs Cokeley just a few days later had more than double the effect. Somehow the murder of a rather unpopular man in a railway carriage several miles away seemed less shocking than the slaying of a woman in her own home right in the middle of the village.

The charging of West with Cokeley's murder had had the effect of restoring a degree of normality to the village. 'That West fellow will hang for sure,' said one of the public house sages. Another added 'I always knew old Goggins was innocent,' and the fact that he had bet several shillings on his guilt was forgotten about.

This time, however, an atmosphere of foreboding lay over the village. Elderly spinsters refused to venture out alone, farmers oiled and checked their shotguns. Doors which were rarely locked were now bolted and barred as night fell. The tea room and the pubs were full of whisperings of crimes far worse than ordinary domestic murder. Some thought it was the work of Irish Republicans, others imagined a network of Bolshevik spies waiting to rise up and slaughter the middle classes at a secret signal from Moscow.

Mr Eustace, the minister of the little Methodist chapel, had blamed the first murder on the incursions of the modern world into the countryside. He linked the killing to the deleterious effects of jazz, motor cars and the cigarette habit amongst women. Now, however, he spoke in low tones of 'dark forces'. He called a special service to entreat the protection of the Holy Spirit upon the village, to include refreshments and a retiring collection for the Fabric Fund.

Some, however, were not overly displeased by the disruption; since Mr Cokeley's murder and the arrival of the gentlemen of the press into the town, the landladies and publicans of the village had not seen such profits since the war, when their establishments had been filled with soldiers from the nearby training camp.

This time the incomers had not worn khaki nor carried rifles, but wore belted raincoats and carried notebooks and cameras. They had promised the village's more attractive young women that their pictures (accompanied by their thoughts on the recent murders) would appear on the front page of the *Daily Mail* or the *Daily Sketch*.

Now that there had been a second murder, some of the more enterprising people of the village braced themselves for more such visitors.

Shaw, who with his clerical collar had been seen emerging from Cokeley's antique shop by the journalists, was easily identified by them. He dealt as politely as he could with the steady stream of reporters who knocked at the door of the vicarage that afternoon and evening, or who telephoned from as far afield as London and Manchester, but after a while he reluctantly had to instruct Hettie to break the Ninth Commandment and inform callers that, unless they were parishioners, he was Not At Home.

He felt somehow that the hour of reckoning was approaching, and he needed a time of quiet to gather his thoughts and pray for guidance on what to do next.

The quiet time did not last long. Shortly after dinner, Shaw was in his study attempting to deal with some administrative matters of the parish, which he had neglected during the excitement of the last few days. He heard an insistent ring at the doorbell and then Hettie's voice loudly admonishing whoever it was who had called.

Good old Hettie, thought Shaw; she had started off seeming to be something of a shy and innocent girl, but the last few days had revealed her to be a highly resolute door-blocker. She was wasted in a country parsonage, thought Shaw with a smile, and would be of more use in a house which lived in constant fear of debt collectors.

Hettie's voice was now clearly audible even with the study door closed.

'I don't care,' said the servant. 'Pretending to know the vicar so that you can get a story for your paper, no doubt. I've had this before and I'm not falling for it again.'

The caller said something inaudible and Hettie replied reluctantly.

'Alright. Wait here.'

There was a knock at the study door. 'Enter,' said Shaw, and Hettie came in, giving her usual token bob.

'I'm very sorry sir,' she said, 'but there's a…man to see you. He says he knows you but I can't see how he possibly can, a flash sort like that.'

'Does he have a name, this flash individual?' asked Shaw.

'Says his name's Davis.'

'That is quite alright Hettie. Please show him in.'

'Well…if you say so, sir,' said Hettie doubtfully, as she withdrew into the hallway.

A few moments later Shaw and Davis were talking as they sat in the two small armchairs by the little fire in the study.

'We meet under rather less covert circumstances than last time, Mr Davis,' said Shaw. 'Would you like tea? Or something stronger, whisky, perhaps?'

'No thanks reverend,' said Davis, who was looking around him uncomfortably. 'I've never been in a vicar's house before. It's not quite what I expected.'

'What exactly were you expecting?' asked Shaw as he filled his pipe.

'I dunno,' replied the estate agent. 'Lots of crosses on the walls and pictures of saints everywhere I suppose.'

'The Reformation rather put paid to that sort of thing,' said Shaw, as he puffed clouds of fragrant smoke into the air. 'We clerics now live much as other men. Sometimes a little too much as other men.'

'No harm in that,' said Davis. 'Nice house in the country, pipes, whisky, servants opening the door, it's not a bad life. I might even take the preaching game up myself,' said Davis with a nervous laugh.

'Forgive me Mr Davis,' said Shaw, 'but I suspect you did not come here to discuss the living standards of the clergy. May I help you with anything?'

'You're right. Matter of fact I will take a glass of whisky if there's one going. I could do with it after the day I've had. Another blooming murder on our doorstep, it's enough to scare anyone out of his wits.'

'Certainly,' said Shaw. 'As you say, it has been a rather unusual day.' He poured two glasses of blended whisky

154

from a bottle on a tray in the corner of the room. 'Soda, or just as it comes?' he asked.

'Straight up, please reverend,' said Davis.

Shaw handed the glass of whisky to Davis who raised it. 'Well here's how,' he said. Shaw silently raised his glass in return and two men drank.

'Thing is, said Davis, 'I wanted to talk to you again about the murder, or murders, I should say. I was a bit cagey about it last time but today, I said to myself, Joe, it's your civic duty. Hold your head up high and visit the vicarage like an honest man.'

'I don't quite follow. What exactly is your civic duty?'

'To tell you some more about how I think it happened,' said Davis insistently.

'Surely this is a matter for the police?'

'That's just it. After what happened today I can't go to the police without being sure. I needed to run it by you first. As a, what do you call it, a neutral party, so to speak.'

'I see. And what have you discovered?'

Davis drained the last of his whisky and leaned forward. 'I'm even more worried now that Symes is mixed up in this. And Ruth – that's Miss Frobisher. Yes, her and all, I reckon.'

'Why do you think that?'

'Last time we spoke I told you he was thick as thieves with Miss Frobisher. Attractive slim blonde girl. I may be knocking on, reverend, but I can still see that. And the papers say the police are still looking for the mystery blonde woman who disappeared off the train. Then, there's the business with wanting Cokeley's house. Twice he's said he'd be willing to go to any lengths to get his hands on it. Then there's me falling asleep in the railway carriage, giving him time to slip out and do in Cokeley.'

'This much we discussed last time we met,' said Shaw.

'Something else has presumably happened to deepen your suspicion.'

'I'll say it has,' said Davis. 'First it looked like Mrs Cokeley might not be going to sell the place after all. Upping her price and that. Symes wasn't happy about that. Then he and Miss Frobisher went round earlier today to finalise the sale of the shop.'

'Yes, I recall seeing them in the high street.'

'Right. And they both came back all smiles, and he says to me we won't be having any more problems with Mrs Cokeley.

'Then he says let's all shut up the shop and go somewhere to celebrate. Well, I says, who's going to look after the shop? I've got a pile of work to get through. Suit yourself he says, me and Ruth are off, and next minute he's telephoned that place by the station to send a taxi, they both jump in and he tells me he'll see me tomorrow.

'But then later I had the law round the office. Well, I knew something was up as we'd seen police cars and all sorts rushing up the high street with the bells going. Like the General Strike all over again. But blow me, if they didn't come in to the office and say there had been another murder.'

'Mrs Cokeley.'

'Right. This 'tec comes in. A Jock, he was, or Irish, I dunno, they all sound the same to me, anyway, McPherson was his name. He comes in and starts asking if Symes and Miss Frobisher had been to Cokeley's place. I say yes, they had a meeting with her earlier. What time was this? he says, and I say, about 11 to about 12. Then this McPherson says Mrs Cokeley's just been found dead!

'Where are they now?, says this copper, and I say search me, they've gone off for a long lunch somewhere and left me holding the baby, so to speak'.

'Would you like a top-up, Mr Davis?' asked Shaw, pointing to the man's glass.

'Oh, er, don't mind if I do. That's good scotch, that is. Yes I will, thank you.'

While he poured a drink for Davis, Shaw mentally reviewed all that he had heard from the man. He handed Davis the glass of whisky.

'Well, here's how, reverend,' said Davis, raising the glass to eye level.

'Quite,' replied Shaw. He had decided not to have another drink himself.

'You are sure about the time, Mr Davis? They were definitely back in the office by 12?'

Davis thought for a moment before replying. 'Yes, give or take a few minutes. Definitely back by ten past twelve, I remember the time because there was a race on at Doncaster. I had a bob each way on something, what was it, oh yes, Idlewind. You don't happen to have a *Life* lying around, do you, reverend?'

Shaw was puzzled. 'A...life?'

'Yes, you know,' said Davis. 'The *Sporting Life*. It's a paper. So's I can see the result.'

'No,' replied Shaw with a smile. 'I fear you will have to wait until tomorrow for the results. Perhaps we could return to the matter in hand?'

'Ah yes,' replied Davis. 'Sorry. So what do you think? What's going on?'

'Did the detective say anything else?'

Davis thought for a moment. 'Not really. He seemed to lose interest a bit by the time he left. Just said to tell Symes and Miss Frobisher to get in touch with him soon as possible. He wrote a telephone number down. I've got it somewhere. Here, I see you've got a telephone in the hallway, you want I should put a call through now? Spill the beans, I mean?'

Shaw was beginning to find Davis' rapid patter and use of unfamiliar slang a little wearing.

'I do not think that will be necessary,' said Shaw, 'at least not at this juncture.'

'But what do you think? Did Symes do in the Cokeleys? I mean, if he did, we've got to tell the law, surely? What if *I'm* next?'

The man was becoming increasingly agitated, thought Shaw. Perhaps, he wondered, he ought not to have given him that second glass of whisky.

'Calm yourself, Mr Davis,' said Shaw. 'From what you have told me it would be inopportune to speak to either the police or Mr Symes about your suspicions. Mr Symes lives locally, I think?'

'That's right,' said Davis, who appeared to have calmed down a little. 'He's got digs at the George, down the corridor from me.'

'Then I suggest you simply leave him a note informing him that you wish to speak to him on his return. He may perhaps have returned already.'

'What if he's done a bunk?'

'Done a...?'

'Cleared off. Run off to France or something, to lie low.'

'I think that is improbable. But I suggest that if he has not returned by tomorrow morning, you yourself telephone the police and tell them what you know.'

Davis breathed out a long sigh. 'Alright. I think you're probably right. All this murder business and the police hanging round has got me on edge.'

Davis stood up to go and Shaw showed him to the door.

'Well thanks, ' said Davis. 'I can't say you've exactly put my mind at rest but it's done me good to have a chat.'

'You are always most welcome to call,' replied Shaw.

'And do not trouble yourself too much. I have a feeling that matters will be resolved very soon.'

'Had privileged information from Him Upstairs, eh?' said Davis with a grin, as Hettie handed him his hat and raincoat.

Shaw smiled. 'I have been applying reason and logic to the consideration of the problem,' said Shaw. 'And those abilities are given to us by God. So in a sense yes, perhaps I have had privileged information.'

'You've lost me there, reverend,' replied Davis, 'but all the same I'm glad we've had a chat. Good night to you.'

The two men shook hands and Hettie shut the door behind Davis. Shaw, lost in thought, walked back into his study and closed the door behind him.

Chapter Fifteen

The following morning, the inhabitants of Lower Addenham woke to the promise of a fine spring day. Some of the more nervous villagers knelt at the side of their beds to offer humble prayers of thanksgiving for their preservation from murder during the night; most, however, dressed hurriedly and walked briskly to the little newsagent's shop in the high street to buy the morning papers, hopeful that they might see the name of their village in print, perhaps even with a photograph for them to cut out and keep as a souvenir.

Children passing Cokeley's shop on the way to the village school glanced at the building, with its lone policeman guarding the front door, and hurried on, fearful lest the murderer should be lurking there, or worse, that the ghosts of Mr and Mrs Cokeley might rush out to assail them.

Breakfasts of porridge or kippers or bacon and eggs were hurriedly devoured by the journalists in the dining room of the George; pipes and cigarettes were lit, pencils sharpened and mackintosh belts tightened as the little army of reporters prepared to fight for 'scoops' in the village. Although a brief mention of Mrs Cokeley's murder had made some of the evening papers, this was the first opportunity for a full day's work on the story, and it was a story that no paper wanted to miss out on.

Upstairs in the George, in the room in which he lived as a permanent lodger, Davis began to awake from his fitful sleep. Two doors down the corridor, the note he had pushed under Symes' door the night before still lay there, unread.

In the basement of Midchester police station, the spring sunlight shone in shafts through the barred windows set high up in the white-painted brick walls. Cell doors slammed and slop-buckets clanked as the handful of prisoners kept overnight began to rouse themselves after a cold, sleepless night.

Inspector Ludd and Sergeant McPherson were up early, much earlier than usual, determined to get to the bottom of the case. One murder in this part of the world was rare; two in such a short space of time was unheard of; and the last thing they wanted was for Scotland Yard to get wind of it and start interfering.

The morning briefing in the office was over, and the other detectives and some of the uniformed constables began sleepily exiting the station to climb into cars and onto bicycles to carry out their orders for the day. There was work to be done in Lower Addenham; doors to be knocked on and statements to be taken.

Ludd, sitting at the interview table next to McPherson, fingered a small cut on the underside of his chin where he had cut himself shaving. He checked with his finger to see if it had stopped bleeding, and satisfied that it had, he turned to McPherson.

'Nothing from the roadblocks, then?' he asked.

'You already asked me that, sir,' sighed McPherson. 'Pretty much every vehicle that went in and out of the village after we got there was checked, as was everyone getting on the trains. Nothing suspicious turned up.'

'Right,' said Ludd. 'What about those two from the estate agents? Symes, and, what was the other one?'

'Miss Frobisher,' said McPherson, glancing at his notebook. 'Nothing there either. They seem to have disappeared.'

'What do you mean, disappeared?'

'I checked on the addresses his partner gave me last night, but Symes still hadn't shown up at his hotel and Miss Frobisher's landlady said the same thing.'

'I don't like the sound of that.'

'Should we alert the ports, sir?'

Ludd snorted. 'You've been at the cinema too much, son. Do you think every port in the country's going to stop people because some country coppers want to talk to them? I suppose you'll want me to put through a call to Croydon Aerodrome as well.'

'Well...' replied McPherson doubtfully.

'No, that's a wild goose chase,' said Ludd. 'I don't think it's them, and we know it can't be West because he was here.'

'But we know it was'nae some random burglary,' interjected McPherson. 'There were no signs of forced entry and nothing was taken.'

'Exactly,' said Ludd. 'There's got to be a connection. Remember what the vicar told us? He thought there might have been two men running from the train.'

'Aye, I do that, sir,' said McPherson. 'And I looked into it. I managed to get through to Lower Addenham station on the telephone this morning. Took a while but they

162

found that engine driver, Ambler, just arrived for the day. He confirmed he saw a man running from the right side of the train, no' the left'.

'Well it's a pity whoever took his statement originally didn't know his something from his elbow – or his right from his left.'

'Och, it was one of the young coppers,' said McPherson. 'Remember we didn't bother paying the driver much attention because back then we all thought that Goggins was the most likely suspect.'

'And that was another wild goose chase,' said Ludd wearily. 'But it looks like there were definitely two men on the job now.'

'Aye, seems like it could be. Cokeley was a big man, probably no' a pushover. West's a wee runt, and maybe a bit unsure about tackling him on his own, so he got a bit of outside help.'

'You could be right,' said Ludd. 'I've looked up the case files for the original robbery five years ago. Cokeley put up quite a fight.'

'Right,' said McPherson. 'So one of them, maybe West, because he's short and slim, puts on the wig and dress and a scarf over his face, makes out he's Jean Harlow.'

'Who?'

'Blonde American girl in the talkies.'

'Oh, right.'

'Anyway, he manages to get into the railway compartment. Sits in the corner with his face covered, all coy like, then somehow gets Cokeley to drop his guard.'

'Urgh,' said Ludd. 'I don't like to think of it.'

'Then the other fellow climbs in from another compartment, they both overpower Cokeley, stab him, West changes clothes and then they make off in separate directions once the train's stopped at the signal.'

'Hmm, but that means the other man had to be in one of the other compartments on the train.'

'Aye, it does. If the second man got on the train when it stopped, you'd think the driver or the guard would have seen him.'

Ludd rubbed his chin and gazed intently out of the office window at the grimy brick wall opposite. 'But the only other men on the train were Goggins, and we know he's physically incapable of climbing along a moving train; the vicar, and those two estate agents.'

'One of who's gone missing,' said McPherson, 'with an attractive blonde girl in tow.'

'Yes, but Symes and his mate Davis were both at Great Netley station when the train arrived,' said Ludd. 'So it couldn't have been one of them the driver saw running off over the fields, could it? And besides, if it had been one of them climbing along the side of the train, surely the vicar would have seen him going past the window? Or at least the driver or the guard might have noticed.'

'What if the vicar and the train crew are all in it together?' said McPherson, punching his fist into his palm in excitement.

'Oh don't be daft, McPherson,' said Ludd wearily. 'You're Scots, not Irish. What would a parson and an engine driver be conspiring to murder an antiques dealer and his wife for?'

'Aye, I suppose you're right sir,' said McPherson. 'I can see it's most likely it was West and an accomplice that killed Cokeley. But why kill his wife, as well?'

'Who knows?' replied Ludd. 'My guess is they knew Cokeley had an antiques shop and the second man decided he'd see what he could rob from it while his partner's safely behind bars. That way he doesn't have to share out any of the loot. Mrs Cokeley finds him and he ends up killing her.'

'Maybe so, sir,' said McPherson with a sigh. 'It's a rare puzzle right enough.'

Ludd stood up and pushed his bowler hat further back on his head.

'Look. I think we've done enough theorising. We've charged West with Cokeley's murder. There's all the evidence with the bicycle tracks and the money bag for that. He's up before the magistrates tomorrow and then he'll be on remand until his trial at the next Assizes. That means he'll be in Ipswich gaol, most like. So it would make our life a lot easier if we can get him or whoever he's working with charged with Mrs Cokeley's murder as well as soon as possible.'

'Right sir,' said McPherson. 'I'll get him in the interview room for a wee chat.'

'…grant that this day we fall into no sin, neither run into any kind of danger, but that all our doings may be ordered by thy governance, to do always that is righteous in thy sight, through Jesus Christ our Lord. Amen'.

Shaw concluded the collect and read the remainder of Morning Prayer in his somewhat chilly parish church, feeling a little disrespectful as he read the Prayer for the King's Majesty a little more quickly than usual.

He concluded with the Grace, turned to nod to the altar and strode to the west door to greet the three elderly parishioners who had turned up. Morning Prayer was read daily in the church at 8 am by either Shaw or Laithwaite, the curate, regardless of whether anybody was there to hear it, and more often than not there was nobody.

He listened politely to the gossip of the three elderly ladies, who were of course concerned about the recent murders.

'Something must be done about these awful Bolsheviks before they kill us all!' declared Miss Kendrick, smelling faintly of mothballs and gin, as usual. Shaw informed her that the police were doing a sterling job, which seemed to reassure her somewhat.

Once the last parishioner had gone, he walked quickly back to the vicarage. Breakfast was served at 8.30 by Hettie. Although he did not have much appetite this morning, he did not want to keep his wife waiting.

He realised, as he entered the vicarage and smelt the aroma of kippers and toast emanating from the little back kitchen, that he felt a lack of hunger. There was some physiological reason for it, he assumed. It was not fear exactly – fear of sudden death or injury had left him permanently in the war – but perhaps a sense of moral duty waiting to be carried out, which made the body baulk at such luxuries as kippers, toast and Frank Cooper's Oxford Marmalade.

Shaw kissed his wife on the forehead and sat down at the breakfast table.

'Good morning dear,' said Mrs Shaw, who had, as usual, still been asleep when Shaw had risen to say Morning Prayer.

'Good morning, Marion,' said Shaw. 'Now what has Hettie brought us today?' He lifted the cover of the metal serving dish with curiosity. 'Ah, scrambled eggs,' he said, without much relish.

After he had eaten a small amount, Mrs Shaw looked at her husband with wifely concern.

'Are you alright dear? You look a little pale.'

'Quite alright thank you. A little distracted, that is all.'

'I suppose we all are,' said Mrs Shaw. 'This awful murder business. It's all over the papers again today and I dare say it will be on the wireless as well. Absolutely shocking. One hears of that sort of thing in London but not in a place like this.' She offered a little piece of kipper to Fraser, who was sitting at her feet, but he merely sniffed it and settled back down to snooze under the table.

'There is no particular reason why we should be spared from such things here,' said Shaw, looking down at his plate. 'For all have sinned, and come short of the glory of God.'

'Romans. Chapter three I think,' said Mrs Shaw. 'No idea what verse, sorry.'

'Twenty-three' replied Shaw.

'Of course,' replied Mrs Shaw briskly. 'Lucian, are you sure you are alright? You don't normally start quoting the Bible unless there's something particularly important going on.'

Shaw paused for a moment before replying. 'If you were able to persuade someone to seek atonement for a terrible sin, would you attempt to do so, even if it turned out that you were wrong?'

'What a peculiar question,' said Mrs Shaw. 'Is this about something metaphorical, or something real?'

'Sometimes the metaphorical can be more real than the real,' said Shaw.

'I'm afraid I don't quite follow you, Lucian, dear. Oughtn't you to speak to the bishop if you're having some sort of theological problem?'

How was he to ask his wife if she believed he should confront someone he thought responsible for two murders? He realised it was not possible. It would merely frighten her and, at any rate, he hoped that his suspicions were not correct and that such a confrontation would result in, at worst, a law suit for defamation of character. He pushed aside his plate, stood up and kissed his wife again on the forehead.

'Pay no attention, my dear. I was getting far too down in the dumps about things. It is hardly surprising, with all that has happened recently. Now, if you will excuse me, I have some parish visiting to do.'

Mrs Shaw looked at her husband with a puzzled expression, then returned to reading the lurid account of Mrs Cokeley's death in the *East Anglian Gazette.*

Once he was in the hallway and the door to the dining room was closed behind him, Shaw picked up the candlestick telephone and asked the operator to connect him with Midchester police station.

Once he was put through, he asked to speak with Inspector Ludd, but was informed that he was in an interview and that he ought to try again later. Shaw replaced the receiver and filled his pipe, determined to telephone again once he had smoked it.

'What's all this about then?' asked West, as he sat in his usual place at the scarred table in the interview room. 'Thought I was supposed to be going up before the beak today.'

'If by "beak" you mean the magistrate, then that's tomorrow,' said Ludd, looking with distaste at West's appearance; crumpled and unshaven after several nights in the police cells. 'We want to ask a few more questions before you get shipped off on remand.'

'How about a fag first?' said West.

'How about you don't speak unless you're spoken to?'

said McPherson, looking at the prisoner with contempt.

'It's alright, sergeant,' said Ludd. 'I think we can afford our clients a little luxury from time to time.' He gave a Gold Flake cigarette to West and lit it for him. West sucked down the smoke hungrily, then leaned back and exhaled it lazily.

'That's better,' said West. 'Now, what can I help you gents with?'

'Who are you working with?' asked Ludd.

'What are you talking about?' said West, with what seemed to Ludd to be genuine surprise.

'You know what we're talking about,' said McPherson. 'We know there were two of you on the train when Cokeley was murdered.'

'I weren't on the train. And I got an alibi. Them girls at Maisie's place,' said West defiantly.

'Och we've some bad news for you about that, son,' said McPherson. 'We finally got to speak to them and none of them remembered anyone of your description. Said they'd had dozens of men in that night.'

West's face fell but he remained defiant. 'Well, so what if I ain't got an alibi? All you've got on me is, what do you call it, circumstantial evidence.'

'My, my,' said Ludd, shaking his head. 'Sounds like you became a barrack-room lawyer when you were inside. We've already had enough to charge you with and once we've built a case we'll have enough to hang you with, lad, you mark my words. We've got witnesses who've said they saw a man of your description leaving the train.'

Ludd knew that was not strictly true, as the vague descriptions from the train crew and Shaw were unlikely to convince a jury, but he was convinced West was the right man. Who else could it be?, he thought.

'I told you, I want to speak to a lawyer,' said West.

'And we've already told you if the court sees fit to appoint one you'll get one,' said Ludd patiently. 'There's a new Act of Parliament just passed says you'll get one free of charge. But unless you've got five guineas or thereabouts to pay for one before that, you're not getting one anytime soon.'

Ludd noticed that West now looked distinctly uneasy; he was puffing hard on his cigarette, which he then stubbed out fiercely into the tin ashtray on the table.

Ludd sensed his advantage and continued with the attack. 'The tyre tracks on that bike of yours matched those we found by the railway line. The mud on the wheels matches the mud there too. It's a very particular type of mud, apparently. I always thought mud was just mud, but no. There's different types, according to the lab boys, and those two are a perfect match.

'Plus we've got your dabs all over the bike. I reckon that's enough to convince any jury.' Ludd leaned back in his chair and lit a cigarette. He did not offer one to West.

'Alright, listen,' said West. 'About the bike.'

'We're listening,' said Ludd.

West pointed to McPherson. 'When he asked me where I'd got it, I kept quiet 'cos I knew it was probably stolen.'

'You do surprise me,' said McPherson.

'I'm not saying I stole it, am I?' replied West with an angry glare in the Scotsman's direction.

'So what are you saying?' asked Ludd.

'I bought it off a bloke in the street. I knew it had to be nicked 'cos it was so cheap, and Mother said she'd seen him hanging about near the house looking shifty. He only wanted five bob for it. Well I reckoned I'd need a bike, for looking for work, and that.'

McPherson snorted with derision. West ignored the interruption and continued.

'So I nips into the house and manages to borrow five bob from me ma, then I pays the chap and puts the bike in the wash-house. Thought I'd best leave it there a few days in case anybody was looking for it.'

Ludd took a deep drag on his cigarette and thought for a moment before replying.

'Did he give you a name, this chap?'

'Don't be daft,' replied West. 'He wasn't going to do that, was he? I could tell he was itching to get it off his hands as quickly as possible. Looked like he had the devil on his tail.'

'Could you describe him?' asked McPherson, opening a fresh page in his notebook.

'About my age, same height and build I'd say,' replied West. 'Didn't get much of a look at him as he had his cap pulled down and his collar up.'

Ludd now took out his notebook and began leafing through the pages. 'When was this?' he asked.

West paused for a moment before speaking. 'Last Wednesday sometime, after lunch sometime I think. About two o'clock. I remember it as it was after I came back from Maisie's.'

'Where they don't remember seeing you,' said McPherson.

'Alright, I know that, don't I?' said West angrily. 'Anyway, I comes up our street and he's hanging around the back gate. Says do I want to buy a bike? I realised right away it was nicked so I says alright, come in our yard, out of sight, like. I said I'd buy it. He said 'don't leave it around here then, push it into that wash-house,' so I did. Then I popped in to borrow the money off mother. Took a while to persuade her but she coughed up in the end.'

'Did your mother see this fellow?' said Ludd. 'The truth now, lad, we'll find out soon enough if she didn't.'

West looked crestfallen. 'No. She never come out in the yard, she was doing out the front parlour all the time I spoke to her. I came out, paid him his five bob and then he was off like his rear end was on fire.'

'Alright, now think carefully, lad,' continued Ludd. 'Was he carrying anything else, this fellow, when he came into the yard?'

West paused and bit his lip. 'He had some sort of sack, over his shoulder, like.'

'Was he still carrying it when he cleared off?' said Ludd.

'Think so,' said West. 'Although now you mention it when he come in I thought it was full but now that I think of it, when I saw him turn to leave, it looked like it was empty. What's that got to do with anything?'

'Never mind,' said Ludd. 'Right, that's all for now.' He turned to the silent officer by the door. 'Take him back to the cells.'

The constable stepped forward and took West by the arm.

'What's going on then?' asked West. 'Why you asking all them questions about a stolen bike? Thought I was supposed to be in for murder.'

'You are,' said Ludd. 'When that changes we'll let you know.'

Once West had been removed from the cells, Ludd sat back in his chair and rubbed his hands over his face.

'Are you thinking what I'm thinking, sir?' said McPherson.

'If you mean was the bike planted, then yes,' replied Ludd. 'Assuming West's telling the truth, and he doesn't strike me as a very good liar. Sounds like whoever this fellow was who sold him the bike wanted him to be found with it. And wanted him to get his dabs all over the handlebars.'

'Aye,' said McPherson. 'That's what I'm thinking. And I'll bet you that's what the sack was for. Probably had Cokeley's bag in it. While West was inside talking to his ma, he planted that in the wash-house. West's thick as a plank but even he'd be suspicious if somebody asked him to look after a bag full of money.'

'He's certainly no criminal genius,' said Ludd. 'But whoever that man is – or men, I should say, as more than likely there's two of them – are clever.'

'They must have known West had done over Cokeley before and that he'd be the first person we'd pick up,' said McPherson.

'They could'nae just creep in at night to plant the bike in the shed, as West would wonder what the hell it was doing there. No, they had to get him to keep it there and make sure his prints were on it. And that's why when I found the bag it was shoved away under the table at the back. That needed to be a bit harder for anyone to find, so's West didn't spend the money and chuck the bag away.'

'But not so hard to find that it didn't get missed in a police search,' said Ludd.

'West's place in Midchester is'nae far from where the train got stopped,' said McPherson. 'Someone could easily have got there by bicycle, half an hour or so after killing Cokeley. So that fits with the machine getting planted on West early afternoon sometime.'

Ludd stood up, put on his jacket and straightened his tie. 'Right, get down to Railway Cuttings and start asking around if anyone saw this chap with the bicycle. And start asking around the bicycle shops to see if anyone's bought that model recently.'

He looked at McPherson, who was leafing through the contents of a buff manila folder on the table.

'Are you listening to me, sergeant?' said Ludd with annoyance. 'I said get down to…'

'Sorry sir,' said McPherson hastily, scanning the contents of the folder. 'I only just got this in the post this morning, but at the time I did'nae think it was important.'

'What is it?' asked Ludd, craning his neck to look at the sheaf of foolscap papers.

'It's from the fingerprint boys at Ipswich.'

'What do they want? They've already matched the prints on the bike with West.'

'Aye sir. They found several positives on the handlebars of the bike. All nice clear ones of West. They told us that already. And that the rest of the bike looked like it had been wiped down.'

'That ties in with our theory,' said Ludd. 'Probably done by this other fellow while West was inside the house getting the money,' said Ludd. 'Pity, if we'd had any other prints that might have helped us.'

'That's just it sir,' said McPherson with mounting excitement. 'All we wanted was to make sure West had touched the bike and that was the first thing they found out for us. But it says here now they've also found a partial match of another print found on the underside of the handlebars. It took them a while, but they've found a match in the records office.'

Ludd looked down at the neatly typed name and address.

'Well don't just stand there,' he said, taking his bowler hat from under his chair and plonking it onto his head. 'Get a car round the front now.'

'Should we not notify the local station, sir? They're nearer.'

'What?' said Ludd. 'And have some bumpkin constable plod over on his bicycle to make the arrest before we do?'

'Aye, I suppose you're right sir,' replied McPherson. 'I'll get the car ready.'

'And get two of the lads along too. With two murders on our hands I'm not taking any chances of there being a third. Now, get going.'

Before Ludd could leave the building he was stopped by a constable who told him he was wanted on the telephone by a Reverend Shaw.

'What on earth does he want?' muttered Ludd as he picked up the proffered receiver.

'Yes, Mr Shaw?' said Ludd.

He listened for a moment, then replied angrily. 'I'm sorry but I don't have time for your fanciful theories, Mr Shaw. You've been very helpful up to now but I'm about to make an arrest and this really isn't the time or the place. *Good day* to you sir.'

Ludd slammed the receiver back into its cradle with a resounding crash, and hurried out into the yard, muttering again under his breath. This time it was something about 'interfering amateurs.'

Chapter Sixteen

Shaw replaced the receiver and took a deep breath. He decided he had done all he could to alert the Inspector, but to no avail. He left the vicarage and walked purposefully along the high street to the end of the village, past Symes and Davis' little office and toward the last of the houses, a small row of cottages on a ridge close to the railway line.

The fine spring weather had changed, with low grey cloud obscuring the sun, and a chilly breeze waving the daffodils in the grassy banks by the road. Shaw shivered slightly, partly from the cold but also from distaste at what he had to do.

Suddenly he heard the clicking and scraping of metal heel protectors on tarmacadam, and he realised somebody was running along the road behind him. He turned to see Davis, red faced, rapidly approaching him.

'Reverend,' he shouted. 'Stop a minute.'

Shaw stopped and waited for Davis to catch up with him; he then waited a few more moments as the man caught his breath.

'Glad I caught you,' said Davis, taking the handkerchief from the top pocket of his suit jacket, and using it to mop his forehead.

'Got some news for you, about Symes, and the murders.'

'Yes?' replied Shaw, concerned that his carefully wrought theory about the killer might be about to be destroyed.

'Looks like it might be to your advantage. Him and Miss Frobisher are back. They didn't do a runner to Paris or anything like that. They only got as far as Brighton.'

'Brighton?' asked Shaw, in a puzzled tone.

'Yes, you know, seaside holiday place.'

'I am aware of what it is, Mr Davis, but what is the relevance?'

'Well,' continued Davis, whose face had now returned to its usual sallow colour, 'there's me thinking they had something to do with Mrs Cokeley being killed as they disappeared so sharpish, and all the rest of it, what we talked about. But it turns out they couldn't have.'

'Indeed, and why not?' asked Shaw.

'It says in the paper today that the police reckon Mrs Cokeley was killed some time between 12 and 1.'

'What of it?'

'Well…I don't know how exact these things are, I mean, I'm not a doctor, but I think that puts Symes and Miss Frobisher in the clear. See, I told you last night, they were back in the office around 12. But now I think it was more like 11.30. I remember now that I saw them come in and I checked the clock.'

'Another horse race?' asked Shaw with a slight smile.

'Not this time reverend, no,' replied Davis, with slight impatience. 'I was a bit hungry and I was hoping it was lunchtime. So anyway, I don't see how it could have been them. And from what they told me today it all made sense anyway.'

'Your suspicions are allayed?' asked Shaw

'No, they've all gone,' replied Davis. 'I thought they

were thick as thieves those two, what with her going on about "extracurricular activities" and him saying nothing was going to stand in his way to getting Cokeley's house. I started to think Joe, old chap, there's something funny going on here. And then when they disappeared after Mrs Cokeley got herself killed, well that was the final straw for me.'

'And that is when you came to me last night with your suspicions.'

'That's right. But you can imagine how daft I felt this morning when they turned up in the office. Seems they had a long lunch to celebrate Mrs Cokeley agreeing to sell the house. One thing led to another and they ended up on the late train to Brighton. I won't say any more but you're a man of the world, I'm sure reverend, so you can imagine what the extracurricular activities were.'

'I would hope that I am in the world but not of it, as St Paul puts it,' said Shaw.

The mention of the seaside resort reminded him, coincidentally, of another part of his theory on the murders, and he resolved he must now take what he hoped would be the final step in his investigation.

'I am aware,' he continued, 'of Brighton's reputation for, shall we say, discreet liasons.'

'But that's just it,' said Davis, beaming. 'That's why I said it could be to your advantage. It's not a discreet liason as you call it, they came back on the early train this morning and they've only blooming gone and got engaged! So you'll be doing the honours soon I hope.'

'Please offer them my congratulations,' said Shaw with relief, 'and tell them that I look forward to meeting with them at the vicarage if they wish to discuss the arrangements.'

'I will, but I'd best be getting back. Symes has left me to

try to make sense of Ma Cokeley's accounts and other things to do with the business. He reckons she was losing money for years. She wasn't too pleased about it either when he told her. That's why she agreed to sell up so easily.'

'I imagine it must have been a strain for her, poor woman.'

'I suppose so, but let's hope she's in a better place now, eh?' replied Davis, with a quick glance upwards. 'Well, I'll say cheer-oh then reverend. I'm glad I got all that off my chest,'.

'That is what I am here for, Mr Davis,' said Shaw. 'Now if you will excuse me, I have some pressing business to attend to.'

'Right-oh. I'll probably be seeing you again soon – he's only gone and asked me to be the best man!'

Shaw raised his hat as Davis turned and trotted back up the road to his office. What a strange little man, he thought.

Shaw knocked on the door of the last cottage, noting the general air of neglect in the tussocky front garden. The door opened a crack and a heavily bespectacled woman's face came into view.

Shaw raised his hat. 'Good day, Miss Ellis. I am calling as promised to see how you are getting on.'

'Really there's no need,' replied Miss Ellis with an irritated tone. 'I'm perfectly alright.'

Shaw smiled, determined not to be put off. 'I have no doubt of that. You are clearly a capable individual. My call was more with regard to the police investigation.'

'Police investigation?' asked Miss Ellis.

'Yes, as the person who found the unfortunate Mrs Cokeley, there will undoubtedly be further questions from the police. It will be in your best interests, I am sure, to be prepared for the sort of questions they may ask, and as someone with a passing acquaintance with the investigating officer, I may be able to assist you in this.'

Miss Ellis continued to look irritated, but her expression softened somewhat. 'You'd better come in,' she said.

Shaw removed his hat and wiped his feet on the mat. Miss Ellis showed him in to the small front parlour.

Shaw looked around the room, with its trappings of down-at-heel, lower-middle-class respectability; the embroidered text on the wall, the anti-macassars on the chairs and the coloured engraving of the King and Queen above the chimney-piece. He noticed a large trunk on the floor with items of clothing half in, half out of it.

'Are you going somewhere?' he enquired, pointing at the trunk.

Before she could reply, there was a thudding on the ceiling and Shaw heard a muffled voice from upstairs.

'Who's that you're talking to Sybil?'

Miss Ellis turned to the doorway of the parlour and called up the stairs. 'It's nothing mother. Just a visitor.'

'If it's the workhouse people you can tell them I shan't come,' she called with feeble defiance. 'I told you, I was born in this house and I'll die in this house.'

Miss Ellis turned back into the room and closed the door. She smiled awkwardly and pushed back a strand of hair. Shaw noticed that despite her dowdy appearance, she was not an unattractive woman.

'I'm sorry about that,' she said. 'We're putting mother in a nursing home. She thinks it's the workhouse. She's getting worse, so we've made arrangements.'

'I am sorry to hear that,' replied Shaw. He looked down at the trunk and the spring frock, silk stockings and fashionable cloche hat on view. 'Forgive me, Miss Ellis, but I cannot help noticing some of the items you are packing. They appear to be more suited to a woman of your own age.'

Miss Ellis folded her arms. 'I...I'll be going to the home myself for a few days to help mother settle in,' she said quickly. 'Look,' she continued, 'what's all this about, anyway? We don't go to your church – mother's a Methodist and I'm, well I'm not really anything anymore and Jack certainly isn't. So I don't see what the point of this visit is.'

Shaw took a deep breath. 'Before I say any more, Miss Ellis, this is a chance for you to unburden yourself of anything that may be troubling your conscience.'

'My conscience? I don't know what you're talking about,' said Miss Ellis, glaring.

'Very well,' said Shaw. 'I will come to the point. I have come here because I believe you to be complicit in the murders of both Mr and Mrs Cokeley. If you come to me now, as your parish priest, with contrition, before we both go to the police, a jury is bound to look more favourably upon you.'

Miss Ellis flushed a deep crimson. 'Contrition? I've no idea what I'm supposed to be contrite about,' she said angrily. 'So why on earth should I go to the police with you or anyone else?'

'Because, Miss Ellis,' said Shaw gravely, 'if you speak now, it could mean the difference between imprisonment, or the hangman's noose.'

'Absolute nonsense,' she snapped. 'They've caught the man who killed Cokeley. The papers said so. They're bound to catch whoever killed his wife soon as well.'

She walked over to the trunk and began hurling items into it. 'Now if you'll excuse me,' she said, looking over her shoulder, 'I have things to do.'

'If you don't do it for yourself, Miss Ellis,' said Shaw, 'at least do it for your brother.'

'My brother? What on earth has he got to do with this?'

'There is something the law calls joint enterprise. If two persons are involved in a murder, both may hang, even the one who did not strike the fatal blow.'

Miss Ellis paused, an expression of suspicion on her face. 'What do you know about my brother?'

'You may not be aware, Miss Ellis, but I was travelling in the same train in which Mr Cokeley was murdered. Consequently, I have an involvement in the case beyond that of an ordinary member of the public. It was your brother that first alerted me to the fact that the case was not as straightforward as the police imagined.'

'What...what has he told you?'

'Your brother Jack and I have never spoken,' said Shaw. 'But I noticed him on his bicycle, cycling past the vicarage shortly before I departed on the train for Great Netley last Wednesday. At that time I did not know who he was. But I then saw him returning in the afternoon, after the murder, this time without his bicycle.'

'He...he would have been going to work,' said Miss Ellis. 'He works at the station in Great Netley. He probably had a puncture and left his bicycle somewhere. Yes, I think that's what he told me.'

'I fear not, Miss Ellis. You see, he was not working that day. Wednesday is his day off.'

'Alright, perhaps it is,' said Miss Ellis. 'They're often changing his days off. I still don't see what this has to do with anything.'

'After the day of the murder I took a walk along the road

to Great Netley. I had occasion to notice that there were indications of somebody moving around the signal on the line where the train stopped.'

'What does a train signal have to do with all this?'

'You said yourself you have read the papers,' said Shaw. 'You will know then, that the train stopped at a signal along the line and it was there that the presumed killer made his escape from the train.'

'Alright, I think I do remember something about that. What on earth are you suggesting? That Jack killed Cokeley?' She snorted with derision.

'No, Miss Ellis, I do not think he did. But after speaking with the good men of the Lower Addenham branch railway line, I concluded that it was your brother who used his knowledge as a railwayman to manually change the signal, in order to stop the train in which Mr Cokeley was travelling.'

'I've never heard such nonsense,' said Miss Ellis. 'It's sheer fantasy. You're not a detective, so all I can conclude is you've got carried away with playing at investigating and got everything wrong.'

'It is true I am not a detective,' said Shaw. 'But I have thought over what I have seen and heard many times and it all leads to one conclusion. That it was you who killed both Mr and Mrs Cokeley.'

'You're jolly lucky there's nobody with me to hear that – it's slander. If you think that I killed them why on earth don't you telephone for the police this instant and have me taken away? There's a box in the lane. I shan't mind in the least, as I'll enjoy seeing you made a laughing stock. I might even sue you.'

'Do you think that such a possibility did not occur to me, Miss Ellis?' asked Shaw. 'That is why I am still giving you the opportunity to give yourself up. But I see you are still reluctant, so may I go on?'

'If you must. I really ought to know what I'm supposed to have done, after all.'

'If you have read about the case you will remember,' said Shaw, 'that an attractive young blonde woman was seen entering the compartment of Mr Cokeley at Lower Addenham. But when the train arrived at Great Netley, she was nowhere to be seen.'

'I remember something about it. The papers said when this chap, what's his name, West, got in and murdered Cokeley, he killed her as well and dumped the body somewhere. Or she went mad with shock and ran away.'

Shaw shook his head. 'No, Miss Ellis. I do not believe the lurid theories of the newspapermen. Nor do I believe the equally lurid theory of the police, that the woman was in fact West, in disguise.'

'What on earth…you mean, they think he disguised himself as a woman? Well, it makes as much sense as anything else you've said,' replied Miss Ellis with a hollow laugh.

'I believe the truth to be far more prosaic. I believe that the mystery blonde woman was in fact, you. You knew of your employer's predilection for attractive women and so you made yourself look as glamorous as possible, as you knew the only person who would be able to gain access to Mr Cokeley's compartment would be just such a woman.'

'Go on'.

'I believe that you then killed Mr Cokeley, after which your brother stopped the train at the signal. When he did so, you quickly removed your dress, wig and shoes, opened the compartment door and gave these to your brother along with Cokeley's money bag. He then fled, pausing only for a moment to release the signal while under cover of the bushes. As it was assumed by the train crew that he was just a fare dodger, the train continued on.

'Your brother then got on his bicycle, making sure that visible tyre tracks were left on the muddy path, and cycled into Midchester.'

'Oh yes, and what was the purpose of that? Or have you finally lost leave of your senses?'

'No, Miss Ellis. I am all too sane, I fear. The purpose of going to Midchester was, I believe, to plant the bicycle and the money bag at the home of the man you knew would be the prime suspect, because he had already carried out a similar robbery – one Reginald West.'

'And how exactly was I supposed to know who he was and where he lived?'

'By reading of him in the newspaper report of his release. I noticed it because it had been used to wrap the items belonging to Mr Goggins which came from your shop, and I assumed you must also have seen it.'

'How can you possibly come up with such a preposterous theory as that?'

'Because, Miss Ellis, I saw the man I now realise was your brother returning to Lower Addenham without his bicycle, looking distinctly perturbed. I knew that had to be significant. One thing the papers did not mention was that he dropped the bag containing the wig and clothes. I know this because it was I who found it. I imagine that was a mistake, and that he intended to dispose of it later.'

'The way you are talking, I'm surprised you didn't think it was some sort of…double bluff. I'm beginning to think you're not all there.'

'I believe that the original purpose was to destroy the wig and clothes so that the "mystery blonde" in the railway carriage would remain a mystery. But in the end it did not matter that the wig and clothes were found, because the police, who perhaps have a little more experience of worldly matters than myself, believed they were used by a man to disguise himself as a woman, which had the effect of throwing them off the scent.'

'Aren't you forgetting something?' said Miss Ellis. 'If I really was in the railway compartment and killed Cokeley, how on earth did I manage to get off the train without being seen by anybody?'

'That was, I admit, something which quite baffled me,' said Shaw. 'But as a biblical scholar, I am aware that different people may give different accounts of the same event. The four gospel authors, for example. In this case, the difference in account, though slight, was crucial, and it was not given by Saint Matthew nor Saint Luke, but by Bill Watkins and Percy Ambler.'

'I've no idea who they are but I'm sure you're going to enlighten me.'

'They work for the railway,' said Shaw. 'Myself and Mr Watkins, the guard, saw your brother running from the left hand side of the train as one faces the engine. Mr Ambler, the driver, reported something similar to the police, but it was not until I spoke to him that I realised he had not seen a figure on the left hand side of the train, but on the right. The police did not notice this anomaly, but I did. Mr Ambler described a slightly built, short man in working clothes, running over the fields towards Lower Addenham.

'That was not, I believe, a man, but you. I suspect that your brother handed the men's clothes to you when the train stopped, you hurriedly changed and passed your wig and dress to him.

'It was he who shouted and banged the door on the left hand side of the train as a distraction while you made your escape. Thus the mystery blonde was enabled to disappear into thin air.'

'Alright,' said Miss Ellis, glowering. 'Assuming this nonsense is true, if I did do all this, what on earth was my motive for it? There were only a few pounds worth of takings that day. It was hardly worth bothering to go to the effort of murdering someone. And you haven't even explained how Mrs Cokeley comes into all this.'

'I admit your motive was difficult to ascertain, but it became more clear after you made several mistakes. Your first mistake was taking the bayonet that belonged to Mr Goggins'.

'How on earth can you prove I took it?'

'I cannot, conclusively. But you will recall that I was in the antiques shop on the day of the argument between Mr Cokeley and Mr Goggins. The bayonet was a particular point of discussion. Upon leaving the shop, Mr Goggins gave the entire box of antiques to me, but when I examined the contents later, the bayonet was not there. Since only myself, Mr Goggins, Mr and Mrs Cokeley and you were in the shop, it could only have been one of us who took it.'

'Exactly,' said Miss Ellis. 'Try proving it was me in a court of law. It could have been any one of us.'

'That is unlikely,' replied Shaw. 'The police did in fact raise the possibility of my own guilt in the matter – but what would have been my motive? Mr Goggins has been ruled out on grounds of disability. Mrs Cokely is now dead, so even if she killed her husband, there is still another killer at large.

'And you are right, Mr Cokeley could have taken the bayonet – he was perhaps concerned about the release of West, and took it for protection; a struggle ensued and the weapon was taken from him and used against him by West.'

'I should say that's a far more convincing explanation than that I did it.'

'Perhaps, Miss Ellis,' said Shaw, 'but it does not explain who killed Mrs Cokeley. That could not have been West, as he was in a police cell when it happened.'

'It must have been someone else working with him, then,' said Miss Ellis angrily. 'I've already told this to the police – the real police – they should speak to that pair from the estate agents who were in the shop just before I found Mrs Cokeley.'

'That, I believe, was your second mistake,' said Shaw.

Before Miss Ellis could reply, there came a thudding noise from the ceiling and the sound of a muffled voice.

'Ought you to attend to your mother?' asked Shaw.

'She can wait,' said Miss Ellis. 'I want to know what mistake you think I made.'

'You attempted to throw suspicion onto Mr Symes and Miss Frobisher from the estate agency, by telling the police they arrived around twelve and were still there when you left. But a witness saw them returning to their office well before twelve. Either the police did not notice this, or they did and intend to pursue the matter.'

'I don't see what that proves.'

'In itself, very little. But the police doctor estimated the time of Mrs Cokeley's death was around noon.'

'I daresay these estimates can be inaccurate,' said Miss Ellis airily. 'And you're forgetting, I wasn't in the shop between twelve and one so how could I have done it?'

'You told the police you were sitting on the bench in Back Lane. A bench that is conveniently secreted from the main highway, and which is not overlooked. And your only witness was…your brother.'

'Got it all worked out, haven't you?' said Miss Ellis, pushing back a lank strand of hair from her forehead. 'There's just one problem – none of it is true.'

'Miss Ellis,' continued Shaw 'you have attempted to

deflect blame for your actions from the beginning; first by making it appear that West was involved, secondly by using the bayonet that implicated Mr Goggins, and finally by claiming that Mr Symes and Miss Frobisher were in the shop when they were not. I am asking you, as your clergyman, to give yourself up before it is too late.'

'You're not my clergyman,' hissed Miss Ellis. 'Mother might fall for all that but I don't. You're all the same, you men. You think you can just cajole me into whatever you want. Taking advantage of your position.'

'On the contrary Miss Ellis,' said Shaw. 'I have sought to use my position to *your* advantage – but I see that my efforts have been in vain. I regret that you leave me no alternative but to speak to the police.'

Shaw strode out of the parlour into the little hallway. The vestibule was silent, except for the distant sound of a car engine straining up the hill from Midchester. Shaw turned to the door, but Miss Ellis deftly blocked it. Shaw noticed a strange gleam in her eyes, perhaps merely the reflection of light from the little window above the door onto her spectacles.

'Wait,' she said. 'I want to know why you think I supposedly did all this.'

Shaw sensed an advantage and pressed it home. 'Very well. I suspect that you were defrauding Mr Cokeley, and that somehow he found out.'

'And how did you work that out?'

'Another mistake, Miss Ellis, was to alter the prices on the items in the shop. The painting that my wife bought, for example. She mentioned a similar mistake had occurred before. Once might have been accepted as human error, but twice aroused suspicion. My wife is rather astute in matters of finance and tends to notice such things.

'You also mentioned to me that on the day of Mr

Cokeley's murder, you had given him a normal week's takings. When the police found the bag, it contained over seven pounds. Mrs Cokeley, however, told me that the shop barely made more than a couple of pounds a week. This added to my suspicions that you were involved in some form of embezzlement.

'I believe that Mr Cokeley found out about this embezzlement, and threatened to expose you. Later on his wife became suspicious as well, probably because of certain allegations that the estate agents were making about her accounts.'

Miss Ellis was silent. She was breathing heavily and staring at Shaw with that same strange gleam in her eyes. Before she could reply, there came again the sound of banging from the ceiling. Shaw stepped forward towards the door.

'Ignore it,' snapped Miss Ellis. 'I've had just about enough of her. Treating me like a servant, at her beck and call, making me pay for doctors when most of the time there's nothing wrong with her.'

'Doctors are expensive,' said Shaw. 'A jury would understand that a person might be driven to extreme measures to pay for one.'

Miss Ellis advanced towards Shaw. He stepped backwards in the direction of the kitchen.

'Clever, aren't you?' said Miss Ellis. 'Alright, between you and me, I'll admit it. I was taking money from Cokeley. And yes, it was to pay for mother's blasted medical bills and to eventually get her off my hands. Jack helps a little but it's not enough.'

'I suspect there was more to it than that,' continued Shaw. He stepped backward into the little kitchen, noting the back door into the garden. He wondered if he could escape throught it, then cursed himself for cowardice.

'I think,' continued Shaw, 'that Mr Cokeley used the threat of exposing you as a thief for his own selfish ends. He became aware that you were stealing from him, but rather than dismiss you, he allowed you continue with your trick of overpricing articles, and any other methods you had such as false accounting. After all, it was making money for him which his wife did not know about. I believe he allowed you to continue with this deception – on one condition.'

'And what was that?'

'On his person the police found a letter from an hotel in Brighton confirming a reservation for a Mr and Mrs Brown. I fear, Miss Ellis, that you were 'Mrs Brown'.

'That was the last straw,' hissed Miss Ellis. 'I put up with him pawing and prodding me, me with no chance of finding a decent man in this godforsaken hole, spending all my time and money looking after mother.'

'So he made you his mistress.'

'No he damned well didn't! He thought he was going to, booking his dirty weekend in Brighton and telling me if I didn't come along he'd tell the police all about me. I pleaded with him not to, I told him I had to take the money for mother's doctors and that I would pay him back. But he wasn't have any of it, oh no. He even had the gall to give me some money himself. Licking his fat fingers and peeling off pound notes with a leer as if he was putting them on a horse at the races.

'He said "don't spend it on your mother dear, buy yourself some decent frocks and get your hair done like those girls in the pictures. Stop being such a frump and show yourself off", he said. The filthy pig.'

Shaw realised the woman was becoming hysterical. He resolved to calm the situation.

'Miss Ellis, forgive me. It was wrong of me to pry. I have

191

perhaps allowed my imagination to run away with me.' He turned towards the back door. 'I shall disturb you no further.'

Before he could place his hand on the door latch, Miss Ellis grabbed a knife from beside the kitchen sink and held it in front of her.

'You're not going anywhere, vicar,' she hissed, with a sarcastic emphasis on the final word.

Shaw breathed deeply. The war had largely cured him of any fear of his own mortality. His concern was more that Miss Ellis would herself be harmed should he attempt to subdue her.

'My dear Miss Ellis,' he said calmly. 'I have no concern for my own safety. But if you harm me it will merely harm your own cause.'

'What cause?' asked Miss Ellis, with a confused expression. 'I tell you, I didn't do anything!'

As she began to advance towards him with the knife in her outstretched hand, Shaw suspected the woman had taken leave of her senses. He realised he must keep her talking until he could summon help.

'Is that how you killed Mrs Cokeley?' he asked gently. 'With a kitchen knife?'

Miss Ellis laughed, and in it Shaw heard an echo of insanity. 'Oh no,' she said. 'It was some sort of antique paper knife lying around. To be honest I didn't expect it to be so sharp. I thought it would just quieten her, not kill her.'

'Quieten her?'

'Yes, she kept on and on at me that day...she said she'd spoken to the estate agents, that there were certain anomalies in the accounts, and that she knew it must be something to do with me. Then she accused me of...of...'

Shaw noticed Miss Ellis's outstretched arm dropping

slightly. He stepped forward slightly.

'She accused you of being her husband's mistress.'

'Get back!' shouted Miss Ellis, and advanced on Shaw, until his back was almost touching the kitchen door. He could feel the little metal latch brush against the fabric of his raincoat.

'Yes,' she continued. 'And that's when I stabbed her. I had to shut her up and stop her saying those filthy things. Just like I had to shut her husband up.'

'I am sure that you did not intend to kill Mr Cokeley,' said Shaw. 'I think you were driven to it. The police will understand.'

'Of course I didn't intend to kill him,' said Miss Ellis. 'Do you think I'm some sort of murderer? We planned just to rob him. Jack and I. Once Cokeley found out I'd been taking money I knew the game was up. That last thirty pounds was enough to get mother into a nursing home and for us to clear out of here.'

'Thirty pounds?'

'Yes, you may be clever vicar, but you don't know everything. There was thirty pounds in Cokeley's bag when he got on the train. We'd had a good week, with my little pricing errors pushing the profits up nicely. The plan was simply to rob him of it. Jack was supposed to leave two pounds in the bag – enough to prove West was the thief – and bring the rest home. But he told me he got muddled and left seven instead.'

'When he planted it in West's yard.'

'Yes. And we used the rest to secure mother's nursing home place. I read about West being released and thought it would be the perfect opportunity to throw suspicion onto him. Jack came up with the idea of planting a bicycle in West's house and stopping the train at the signal was his as well. Clever, wasn't it?'

Shaw noticed the woman's arm was now almost by her side. He continued to engage her in conversation.

'And yet you did kill Mr Cokeley. Some might say you planned it, since you took Mr Goggins' bayonet with you on the train.'

'That was only to scare him,' said Miss Ellis. 'I thought of that on the spur of the moment when I was packing the bayonet away. I thought I'd get dressed up in those ridiculous clothes and wear a wig to make my hair look like those silly women in the films. The way he wanted it.

'He didn't recognise me at first when I got into the compartment as I had a scarf around my face and was wearing dark glasses. But once the train got underway he did. He thought I'd actually gone along with his scheme to make myself look like a tart at his expense.'

'And he took advantage of the situation.'

'He tried, the beast. I knew I just had to keep him occupied for a few minutes until the train stopped. We'd timed it the week before and I knew exactly when we'd get to the signal. But that brute couldn't keep his hands off me, he started talking nonsense about leaving his wife and setting me up as some sort of kept woman, and the train wasn't stopping and I...I stabbed him to make him stop. To make it all stop.'

Shaw felt a wave of pity for Miss Ellis; her previous air of defiance had been replaced by one of defeat and despair.

Shaw realised this was his chance, and he lunged forward to grab Miss Ellis' wrist. With surprising force she attempted to wrench her arm free.

'I...told...you,' she gasped, 'You're not going anywhere!' Her arm shot free of Shaw's grip and she raised it high; a ray of sunshine from the kitchen window behind her gleamed momentarily off the blade. Time seemed to stand still and Shaw realised with a strange calmness that this was the hour of his death.

Suddenly he heard someone shouting from the passage in front of him, from behind Miss Ellis.

'Stop, Sybil. No more killing.' It was her brother.

Miss Ellis looked around in confusion, and lowered her arm.

'What...what are you doing Jack? Why aren't you at work?'

Ellis stepped forward. 'Don't come any closer!' said his sister, turning between her brother and Shaw, holding the knife in front of her. 'Or you, vicar.'

'It's all over, Sybil,' said Ellis, gently. 'The police are here. I've told them everything.'

'Everything?' asked Miss Ellis, plaintively.

'I told them how I planned the robbery with you, for mother's sake. And that when Cokeley got stabbed, well, I kept quiet about that as I know why it happened. But when Mrs Cokeley got killed too, well, there was no justification for that, was there? And now the vicar? You ain't in your right mind, Sybil. You need help.'

'I don't need anyone's help!' screeched Miss Ellis, and this time she lunged forward towards Jack. Shaw watched as, almost in the manner of a silent comedian slipping on a banana skin, Miss Ellis fell backwards as a strong pair of arms grabbed her through the opened sash window behind her. They were the arms of Detective Sergeant McPherson.

'Drop it Sybil, drop it!' said the Scotsman, and then there was the clatter of metal on stone as the knife fell to the floor. Shaw deftly kicked the weapon away where it spun off along the tiles into the corner of the room.

After a brief struggle Miss Ellis went limp, her head nodded forward and she began sobbing. Inspector Ludd stepped into the kitchen from the hallway and placed his hand on her arm. After he had done this, McPherson released his hold on her and came into the kitchen via the back door.

'Now come along quietly, miss,' said Ludd. 'We're taking you and your brother in the same car so this will be the last you'll be seeing of each other for a while. Make the most of it, eh?'

Miss Ellis looked at him uncomprehendingly and sniffed back tears, as McPherson led her out through the passageway; a uniformed constable then secured Ellis' hands behind his back with handcuffs and led him out the same way.

'Wait,' exclaimed Shaw. 'Mrs Ellis is in bed upstairs. She is an invalid. I ought to see her.'

'Best leave her out of it for now,' advised Ludd. 'We'll get a constable to stay here and we'll alert the district welfare officer to have her put somewhere.'

Shaw exhaled. 'Very well. But how did you know to come here?'

'I might ask you the same question, Mr Shaw,' said Ludd, pushing his bowler hat back slightly on his forehead.

'I had only a theory, but it seems I was correct,' replied Shaw.

'From what I heard out in the corridor, you worked things out fairly well,' said Ludd, in a tone of grudging admiration.

'You were listening?' asked Shaw in amazement.

'For most of the time, yes. We saw you talking through the window when we arrived and I told McPherson to stop out there while I came in the front with Ellis. Fortunately the front door was unlocked.'

'But why did you not intervene earlier?' asked Shaw.

'You were doing a pretty good job of extracting a confession from her, that's why,' replied Ludd. 'I doubt she'd have been as co-operative with us as she was with you. I can see you have a way with people.'

'Perhaps, Inspector. But I still don't understand, how did you know Ellis was involved?'

'If you'll forgive me, Mr Shaw, it's because we're professionals and you're an amateur. You might have reached the same conclusion as us on theory, but we got there on hard evidence.'

'Evidence?'

'Fingerprints, to be specific. After some considerable effort, a print belonging to Ellis was found on the bicycle he planted on West. Ellis' prints are fortunately on central county files for an arrest on a minor charge some while back.'

'Ah yes...drunk and disorderly, I believe,' said Shaw. 'Now that I recall, Ellis' superior at Great Netley station mentioned it.'

'My my, Mr Shaw, you have been busy,' said Ludd. 'We had his case details which mentioned that he worked at Great Netley station, so we picked him up straight away. He told us everything there and then, as if he couldn't wait to get it off his chest, so we came here to pick up his sister. I brought him in with me in the hope of getting her to incriminate herself in front of him, but since you were doing such a good job of that I told him to keep quiet and wait in the passage.'

Shaw sighed. 'Will the confession be sufficient for her to be found guilty?'

Ludd sniffed. 'Not for me to say, sir. But a double murder? It looks likely she'll hang. We just heard earlier that the fingerprint boys found a partial print on the handle of the knife that Miss Ellis used to kill Mrs Cokeley.

It looks like she had the presence of mind to wipe it, but once we've taken her prints I'm pretty sure we'll find a match.'

'And what of, what was his name, West? The man falsely arrested.'

'We'll have to let him go,' said Ludd, 'but I daresay we can nab him again for receiving stolen goods, or some such. I wouldn't lose any sleep over him, sir. Nasty piece of work.'

'I see,' said Shaw. 'I assume you will require me to make some sort of statement at the police station?'

'If you would be so kind, sir,' said Ludd. 'And may I also say, perhaps I was a bit harsh with you on the telephone today. You've done us a service here today and risked your own neck doing it. It's been a tricky case this, and I appreciate your efforts. So please accept my apologies for any offence given.'

'None taken, Inspector,' replied Shaw.

Chapter Seventeen

Easter came and went, then Whitsun, and finally the church calendar settled into the lull before Advent known as Ordinary Time, when the absence of major festivals meant Shaw could afford himself a little more leisure time.

It was a fine summer morning and Shaw was at the dining table after having read Morning Prayer, finishing his second cup of English Breakfast tea after an excellent plate of kippers. Fraser, as usual, sat nearby, hoping to receive crumbs from the table. The room was silent except for the dull rhythmic thud of the little dog's tail upon the Persian carpet.

There was a rattle at the front door and a few moments later, Hettie entered the room, bobbed, and held out to Mrs Shaw a silver tray with some letters on it.

'Post's come, ma'am', she said brightly.

'Thank you Hettie,' said Mrs Shaw. 'Please clear away the breakfast things.'

'Yes ma'am,' said Hettie. She bobbed again and clattered the plates and dishes into a large pile on a tray.

Once the servant had left the room, Mrs Shaw turned her attention to the post. 'I don't recognise the writing on this one,' she said, peering at a semi-legible scrawl on a brown envelope. 'I do hope it's not another of those odd crank letters we got a few weeks ago.'

'We should not judge them as cranks, my dear,' said Shaw. 'They were people with over-active imaginations who formed a view from reading the newspapers that I was some sort of consulting detective.'

'Well you did do a jolly good job on that case,' said Mrs Shaw. 'I doubt Inspector Ludd and his men would have noticed some of the things you did.'

'Perhaps not. But let us pray there are no more unfortunate people who believe that they require some sort of clerical version of Sherlock Holmes.'

'That fellow that used to be in the *Strand* magazine?' asked Mrs Shaw. 'Oh yes, I've heard he's rather good. Anyway, I assume you've seen the article in the *Times*?'

'About poor young Ellis being sentenced?'

'I'd hardly call him poor, dear. He did after all take part in a killing with his sister, even if he claims they didn't plan to murder him.'

'I believe him,' said Shaw. 'I am only sorry that I was not able to help him more.'

'You did your best dear, you must have visited him at least half a dozen times and you even wrote to that barrister in London. And you managed to get poor old Mrs Ellis that place in the almshouses. You can be quite sure you went the extra mile.'

'I suppose so,' said Shaw. 'Still, fifteen years' hard labour. It will break him.'

'He was lucky not to be hanged,' said Mrs Shaw briskly. 'And so was his sister.'

'Miss Ellis has been committed to a hospital for the criminally insane, probably for the term of her natural life,' said Shaw. 'I would hardly call that luck.'

'Oh dear,' said Mrs Shaw with a sigh. 'Now I've gone

and spoilt your day, by bringing all this up again.'

'Nonsense,' said Shaw. 'And you haven't read that letter. It may be good news.'

'I had quite forgotten,' said Mrs Shaw, looking down at the envelope. 'It's addressed to you, anyway.' She handed it to him.

Shaw opened the envelope briskly using his little finger and scanned the contents.

'Ah,' he exclaimed. 'It's from Mr Davis.'

'Who, dear?'

'You remember. The estates agent. He came here one night, somewhat agitated, with a theory about the murder.'

'Oh yes,' said Mrs Shaw. 'A rather peculiar man. Hettie wasn't impressed by him at all. She told me afterwards that such common types ought not to be allowed in the house.' She laughed and continued.

'She has some rather snobbish ideas, that girl, I must say. I think she must have picked them up when she was working at the Manor. Anyway, what does this Mr Davis want with you?'

Shaw scanned the contents. 'He says he's sorry to disappoint but his business partner Mr Symes won't be getting married here after all. They've all "upped sticks", as he puts it, and moved to Ipswich, where the wedding has already taken place. Apparently there are "rich pickings to be had in the housing game" there. They intend to build along one of the new arterial roads.'

'Oh,' said Mrs Shaw. 'He must be the one who had that office at the end of the high street. I haven't seen anyone in there for an age. Does that mean those awful suburban villas aren't going to be built here? I do hope so.'

Shaw smiled. 'And there were accusing Hettie of snobbery. Perhaps it's you she gets it from.'

'Oh don't be so silly, Lucian,' said Mrs Shaw briskly. 'A dislike of jerry-built houses is not snobbery, it's simply a concern for standards.'

Shaw raised an eyebrow, then continued. 'Mr Davis writes that his firm is not, after all, able to buy the Cokeleys' house and therefore, since the access road cannot be built, they have had to regretfully cancel the plans for the New Addenham estate, and are selling the land back to a local farmer.'

'Oh, that's wonderful news, Lucian,' said Mrs Shaw. 'We've quite enough people living here already. But what will happen to the Cokeleys' house? Does he say anything about that? It's been lying empty for an age.'

Shaw turned over the sheet of lined paper and peered at Davis' indelible-pencil scrawl. 'Good Lord,' he exclaimed.

'You're not usually one for taking His name in vain, dear,' admonished Mrs Shaw. 'What is it?'

'It seems that since Mrs Cokeley died without making a will, the property has reverted to the Crown, which in turn has seen fit to return it to the former owner of the land, which is, the Diocese of Bury St Edmund's. It belongs to the church!'

'How extraordinary,' said Mrs Shaw. 'But what on earth will the church do with an old antiques shop?'

'I have an idea,' said Shaw, standing up and placing his breakfast napkin on the table. 'Do you recall that Mr Goggins was to be turned out of his cottage because he was behind in rent to Mr Cokeley?'

'I think so, yes.'

'He was in very low spirits about this when we spoke last Sunday. It seems that Mr Cokeley's executors are refusing to allow him to stay, and state that the house must be sold to clear various debts.'

'But what has that to do with Mr Cokeley's shop?'

'If the shop is now the property of the church, it may be possible to rent it to Mr Goggins. He could use the shop for his saddlery business and live upstairs. I shall write to the bishop immediately.'

'That's an awfully good idea, Lucian,' said Mrs Shaw. 'You really are very clever about organising these things. Now, I must take Fraser for his walk. He's simply dying to be let out.'

Fraser jumped up excitedly and followed his mistress out into the hallway, where she fussed about with his lead. Shaw kissed his wife on the forehead and patted Fraser's head as the pair left the vicarage.

The house was quiet except for the distant sound of Hettie humming in the kitchen as she washed the breakfast dishes. Shaw walked into his study, closed the door and began to compose a letter to his bishop. A tune came into his head and he realised, again, it was Sandys, *Teach Me My God and King*. How did it go? He sat back and recalled the words.

> A man that looks on glass,
> On it may stay his eye;
> Or if he pleaseth, through it pass,
> And then the heaven espy.

Had he spied heaven in his amateur investigations, he wondered? Not exactly; he had seen the mixture of sin and goodness in all men, but a form of order had been restored, he believed, out of the chaos of sin. Was that order perhaps a glimpse of heaven? Shaw shrugged and decided it was too early for philosophising. He decided to give the good news to Goggins about the shop, and walked out into the warm brightness of the summer morning.

Other books by Hugh Morrison

The King is Dead

An exiled Balkan king is murdered in his secluded Suffolk mansion following a meeting with the Reverend Lucian Shaw. While the police hunt for the sinister agents of a foreign power thought to be responsible, Shaw begins to realise that the killer may be closer to home.

The Wooden Witness

After finding the battered corpse of a spiritualist medium at an archaeological site on the Suffolk coast, the Reverend Lucian Shaw is thrust into a dark and deadly mystery involving ancient texts and modern technology. Was the medium a victim of the evil forces he claimed to have harnessed, or is there a rational explanation for his death?

The Secret of the Shelter

11-year-old Jack and his cousin Ella dare each other to explore the garden of an abandoned London house. They enter a half-buried bomb shelter, untouched since the Second World War, but when leave, they realise they have travelled through time to 1940 – with no way back.

Published by Montpelier Publishing
Order online from Amazon

Printed in Great Britain
by Amazon